ON THE LOOKOUT

LANTERN BEACH P.D., BOOK 1

CHRISTY BARRITT

River Heights

COMPLETE BOOK LIST

Squeaky Clean Mysteries:
#1 Hazardous Duty
#2 Suspicious Minds
#2.5 It Came Upon a Midnight Crime (novella)
#3 Organized Grime
#4 Dirty Deeds
#5 The Scum of All Fears
#6 To Love, Honor and Perish
#7 Mucky Streak
#8 Foul Play
#9 Broom & Gloom
#10 Dust and Obey
#11 Thrill Squeaker
#11.5 Swept Away (novella)
#12 Cunning Attractions
#13 Cold Case: Clean Getaway
#14 Cold Case: Clean Sweep
While You Were Sweeping, A Riley Thomas Spinoff

The Sierra Files:
#1 Pounced
#2 Hunted
#3 Pranced
#4 Rattled
#5 Caged (coming soon)

The Gabby St. Claire Diaries (a Tween Mystery series):
The Curtain Call Caper
The Disappearing Dog Dilemma
The Bungled Bike Burglaries

The Worst Detective Ever
#1 Ready to Fumble
#2 Reign of Error
#3 Safety in Blunders
#4 Join the Flub
#5 Blooper Freak
#6 Flaw Abiding Citizen
#7 Gaffe Out Loud
#8 Joke and Dagger (coming soon)

Raven Remington
Relentless 1
Relentless 2 (coming soon)

Holly Anna Paladin Mysteries:
#1 Random Acts of Murder
#2 Random Acts of Deceit

Suburban Sleuth Mysteries:
Death of the Couch Potato's Wife

Fog Lake Suspense:
Edge of Peril
Margin of Error (coming soon)

Cape Thomas Series:
Dubiosity
Disillusioned
Distorted

Standalone Romantic Mystery:
The Good Girl

Suspense:
Imperfect
The Wrecking

Standalone Romantic-Suspense:
Keeping Guard
The Last Target
Race Against Time
Ricochet
Key Witness
Lifeline
High-Stakes Holiday Reunion
Desperate Measures
Hidden Agenda
Mountain Hideaway

Dark Harbor

Shadow of Suspicion

The Baby Assignment

The Cradle Conspiracy (coming August)

Nonfiction:

Characters in the Kitchen

Changed: True Stories of Finding God through Christian Music (out of print)

The Novel in Me: The Beginner's Guide to Writing and Publishing a Novel (out of print)

PROLOGUE

Tears poured down Moriah Roberts's face as she navigated the island road.

She didn't know if they were tears of joy or tears of fear. Probably both.

This was her chance to start over. For the first time in forever, hope sprang inside her. But she knew that hope came at a cost. She'd given up everything for a chance at a new life.

Not *just* a new life.

A new purpose.

A grin stretched across her face amidst the tears.

Purpose.

Seeing the reason for your existence on the distant horizon wasn't overrated. In fact, purpose could be everything. In recent months, Moriah had been reminded that she was placed here on this earth for a reason.

Not simply to exist. Not to get in the way. Not to be mocked.

She used her sweater to wipe the moisture from beneath her eyes.

Just ahead, she saw her destination.

Her breath hitched with excitement.

The sign was simple—just words carved neatly into wood that read "Gilead's Cove, a Private Community." An iron fence surrounded the whole place, complete with a guard station at the entrance. RVs were laid out neatly in the distance. Beyond the RVs were peaceful water and a few sparse trees. In the center of it all was one permanent structure—a wooden building with some type of tower in the center.

Moriah paused for a moment. The place looked more rundown than she'd imagined. But that was okay. If the Cove were too fancy, it would go against the group's mantra of giving up everything for the cause. These surroundings were humble and the RVs were equalizers, allowing everyone to be on the same level.

She pulled up to an iron gate and pressed a button at the brick guard station that had been built into the fence. A moment later, a man ambled down the path toward the entrance.

He was probably in his fifties and short, with a paunch and saggy jowls. He had only a hint of red hair around the edges of his crown, and he wore khaki pants with a tunic-like beige shirt and sandals.

He climbed into the guard station and opened a small window there to speak with her.

"I'm Barnabas, and welcome to Gilead's Cove. Your name?" His voice had a slight lisp to it.

"Moriah Roberts. You … you should be expecting me." Her voice quivered as she said the words. She knew the people here didn't care about her ratty, twenty-year-old car. They didn't care that she wore an old gray sweatshirt she'd had since she was seventeen. But she still felt self-conscious. The whole world had judged her as trailer-park trash ever since she could remember. Those verbal barbs she'd received weren't easy to shake.

Barnabas checked a list on a clipboard he held in his hands. "As a matter of fact, we are expecting you. Anthony will be anxious to meet you."

Anthony Gilead. *The* Anthony Gilead.

The man … he was anointed. Chosen. Someone who could see into Moriah's soul and knew how to fix all the cracks and breaks. She'd never, ever met anyone like him—someone who filled her with so much confidence that change was possible.

She'd only met him briefly—after she'd heard him speak. He'd prayed over her and then introduced her to some of his leaders, who had nurtured her until she was ready to come here.

"We'll need your phone." Barnabas reached out his hand.

Moriah gave it to him.

"Did you bring anything else?" He glanced into her back seat.

"Just my suitcase. It has clothes and toiletries."

"We're going to need that also. We believe in getting rid of anything that signifies individuality in favor of conformity. It shows we're all equal. We want everyone to understand that no one is more or less important than anyone else."

Equality sounded amazing—especially since Moriah had always been the one who ended up at the low end of the social totem pole. Besides, all her clothes were old and stained. She was ready for a completely fresh start.

Her heart skipped a beat. She couldn't believe she was actually here. From the moment she'd met Gilead, she'd dreamed about this. She'd heard this new community he'd started here was a place of healing, somewhere she could find herself.

She was ready for her life to be simpler. To be filled with the labor of her hands. She looked forward to getting rid of all technology and embracing the life God had designed for her.

As Barnabas opened the gate, Moriah swallowed hard.

And she also hoped that Vince didn't find her here.

No, he wouldn't. She'd be safe here—safely away from Vince and the control he wanted over her.

CHAPTER ONE

Cassidy Chambers's lungs burned, but she couldn't slow down. No, she had to run faster.

Her legs were nearly on fire as her feet dug into the sand.

But no way would she let Ty win this race—not without a fight, at least. He had been a Navy SEAL, so he had an advantage on her.

As their finish line—an old, weathered fence that ran alongside a sand dune—appeared in the distance, Ty seemed to get a burst of energy. He surged ahead and beat her.

A flock of seagulls appeared to celebrate with him by clattering from their place on the beach and soaring in the salty air. Even the waves were crashing especially loud today, as if lending their applause.

Cassidy paused and bent forward, trying to catch her breath. As she did, she cast her husband a loving scowl. "Good job."

Kujo—their golden retriever—barked beside her. The dog didn't look winded at all. Maybe Cassidy needed to up her workout routine.

She still hadn't gotten used to running on the sand. It made jogging ten times more challenging. But Cassidy was always up for a good challenge, especially with Ty by her side.

"Good job." Ty raised his hand to give her a high five. Sweat beaded his face and his thick, dark hair rustled with the chilly ocean breeze. The man looked equally as good in a tux or in running shorts and a tee.

"Uh huh." She was still trying to catch her breath. But she raised her hand, not willing to leave her husband hanging. As their hands connected, Ty caught her fingers in his grip and pulled her closer. His hands went to her waist.

"Have I told you how beautiful you are?" Ty peered into her eyes, his gaze filled with warmth that occupied her dreams at night.

Her heart skipped a beat as she looked up at him. Six months of marriage, and Ty still got her pulse racing and made her feel like the luckiest girl alive. "You're just saying that because you won."

A grin spread across his face. "That's not true."

"Well, you should just be happy that I'm a good sport." She playfully poked his rock-hard abdomen. "Otherwise, I might be bitter right now and hold it against you."

Ty leveled his gaze. "I won that race fair and square."

"I think you've been sneaking in some workouts while I've been on the job."

"I would never …"

Cassidy stepped closer. "It's a good thing I love you."

"Yes, it is, a very good thing." Ty planted a soft kiss on her lips before pulling away and taking her hand. They started back toward their house, just over the dune, with Kujo trotting along beside them.

Just as they stepped onto the deck, Cassidy's phone —snug in a holder strapped on her arm—rang. She pulled it out, glanced at the screen, and saw it was an unknown number from Washington State.

Her pulse quickened.

Washington represented her old life—a life that couldn't materialize here in Lantern Beach. Not if she wanted to stay alive.

"You recognize the number?" Ty asked, looking over her shoulder.

She shook her head. "No, I don't. But what if it's something important?"

"It's your call."

After a moment of hesitation, she put the phone to her ear but said nothing.

Finally, a voice came from the other line. "Cad— Cassidy, I mean. This is your mom."

Cassidy's breath caught. The voice was definitely her mom's—and she sounded frantic. So frantic that she'd almost used Cassidy's old name—the one that could never be spoken again if she wanted to remain safe.

Her mom should know it was too risky to call. This had to be an emergency.

"Is everything okay?" Cassidy rushed.

"It's your father. He's had a stroke."

The wind felt like it had been knocked out of Cassidy. She backed up and leaned against the house to steady herself. "What?"

"He's not doing well. Not at all."

"I'm so sorry to hear that. What's the prognosis?"

"It's going to be a long road, a very long road. He had an ischemic stroke, where the blood flow to the brain is blocked. It's too soon to say how this will affect his speech and movement, but it's going to be a long road to recovery."

"Mom, I'm so sorry. I wish there was something I could do."

"There is something, actually. We need you to take over your father's company. You know it needs to stay in the family—"

Certainly, her mom couldn't be asking that. She should know better, should know what was at stake. "I can't do that. I have to remain in hiding."

"I've thought about the circumstances. But we could protect you. We could hire people. You'd be safe."

"Mom—"

"This is the only solution. Believe me, I've thought through all of them. Just don't dismiss it yet."

"I can't stay on the line, Mom, just in case this is

being tracked." Unlike in the movies, they didn't have sixty seconds before someone could trace her location. But the longer they spoke, the better chance someone had to pinpoint her exact location—if someone was listening.

"I followed all the protocols. But I understand. Please, let me know. This news about your father's stroke hasn't gone public yet, but when it does ..."

After the call ended, Cassidy stood there in stunned silence a moment.

"Cassidy?"

She looked over at Ty and saw the questions in his gaze. "My dad had a stroke."

Ty pulled her into his arms. "Oh, Cassidy. I'm so sorry to hear that. How serious?"

"I don't know if he'll ever be the same, Ty. My mom has never sounded so shaken."

Her mind swirled as her thoughts shifted to her mom's proposition. What was she thinking? Didn't she understand the situation Cassidy was in? Didn't she know that Cassidy never wanted to head up a tech company? She wasn't the right person for the job. She was blood, but blood wasn't enough.

"Did she say anything else?" Ty asked, gently rubbing her back.

"Yes, she did, actually. She said—" But before Cassidy could adequately fill him in, her phone rang again. This time it was dispatch.

This was supposed to be Cassidy's day off. Then again, as police chief, she never really got a day off.

"Hi, Melva," Cassidy answered. "What's going on?"

"I know I'm not supposed to disturb you." Her soft voice cracked, as it always did when Melva addressed Cassidy. "But something's happened, and I really think you should know about it."

Cassidy truly hoped this was important. Last time Melva had started a conversation like this, it was because someone's cat got stuck up in a tree. The fifty-something woman might be a cat lover, but that didn't make it an emergency.

"Go ahead." Cassidy paused by the railing, trying to breathe deeply and comprehend what she'd just learned.

"A dead body has washed ashore."

Cassidy stiffened and glanced at Ty. "A dead body? When? Where?"

"Someone called it in about fifteen minutes ago near Croatan Lane. Officer Leggott went to check it out and confirm the story. It's true."

"We haven't had any reports of any vacationers missing, have we?"

"No, Chief."

"Tell Officer Leggott I'll be right there."

So much for Cassidy's day off. She glanced up at Ty. "We'll talk more later."

Maybe it was better that way. Because she needed more time to think.

———

CASSIDY KNELT on the sand and observed the corpse.

The man was probably in his mid-thirties. He was tall with thick shoulders and an even thicker midsection. His hair was brown and coarse. At one time, his skin had probably been white, but it was now a greenish-black color, wrinkled, and bloated.

If Cassidy had to guess, she'd say the man had been in the water for a couple days. His body was mostly intact, and sea creatures had only begun to eat his soft extremities. If he'd been in the water too long, he would have what was called grave wax.

Cassidy had seen the condition in one other case. When she'd worked back in Seattle, they'd pulled a body from an abandoned swimming pool. The sight had been forever burned into her memory.

The water here on the North Carolina coast was still cold at this time of year—around sixty degrees—which would cause the body to break down more slowly. The cold water also assured that sharks hadn't shredded the body and bacteria hadn't sped up the decomposition process.

Still, this wasn't a scene for the faint of the heart.

Yet the faint of heart were already gathering—innocent beachgoers coming over to see what the commotion was. Crime-scene barricades had been placed around the body so no one could get close—but they could still see plenty.

"Officer Leggott, keep them back," Cassidy said. "We need to put up some screens so people can't see this."

Mostly, Cassidy said that out of respect for the dead. But she had just read about a lawsuit against a small police department where someone had sued for PTSD after seeing a crime scene. It could be beneficial to take precautions.

"Yes, Chief."

Her gaze went to the man's jaw. It was hard to tell with his skin discoloration, but there appeared to be bruising around his neck. Had the man been strangled? Had he died from asphyxiation?

Her initial thought that the man had drowned began to fade. His death might not have been an accident at all.

But ...

She got on her knees and peered closer.

The pattern of bruising seemed to swing upward at the back of the victim's neck. Almost like a noose.

Cassidy might assume that the man had hung himself. But, if that was the case, how had he ended up in the ocean? That didn't make sense.

She pulled on a glove and reached into the man's pockets. They were empty. If no one could ID the man, they'd take his prints and dental records. That way, they'd have them to compare with any missing persons.

Had this been a vacationer whose trip had gone terribly wrong?

It was a possibility.

Though it wasn't a season for going to the beach, many fishermen loved using the island year-round. Some people just came to get away from their everyday lives. Others had second homes here, and they came in the winter to work on renovation projects.

Officer Leggott handed her a blanket. Cassidy draped it over the man. It would offer some privacy until the medical examiner arrived and they could remove the body from the scene.

As she looked across the beach and scanned the spectators there, one man caught her eye. He stood near the sand dune, and he was on his phone as he stared at the scene.

She'd never seen the man before. But that wasn't the reason why he'd caught her eye.

He wore jeans that were stained—dirty with mud, not the normal kind of beach dirty. His flannel shirt was also dirty, as if he'd been doing manual labor or working outside.

Strange.

Something about him just seemed out of place here.

With Leggott guarding the scene, Cassidy took a step toward the man near the dune.

But, in the blink of an eye, he'd disappeared.

Cassidy stared, wondering if she was missing something. But the dune was empty, like he'd never been standing there.

Strange. Very strange.

She should have known better than to think things would stay peaceful here on Lantern Beach for long.

CHAPTER TWO

"So how are things going at Hope House?" Wes O'Neill asked.

Ty gripped the steering wheel of his restored antique Chevy truck, affectionately named Big Blue, and glanced over at his friend. They were headed to the store to get some plumbing supplies for one of the small cabana-like cottages they were building on the back of Ty's property.

"We had our first six-week session, and it couldn't have gone better." The place was an answer to prayer. Ty felt called to help other SEALs who'd returned from battle with wounds—both invisible and visible.

That was why he'd started Hope House. He'd transformed his grandfather's old cottage into a retreat center where wounded military veterans could come to heal.

However, a huge nor'easter had come through in February and ripped the roof off a couple of their new buildings. Even though they had funding for the initial build, their expenses were racking up again. Ty worried the financial strain could affect his marriage—and that was the last thing he wanted.

"When's your next session?" Wes glanced over at Ty.

His friend was a part-time plumber and a part-time kayak guide. Most people around here had to work more than one job to make ends meet, and Wes was no different.

With his nearly shaved head and lean frame, Wes seemed to be living his dream life. The man had intelligent eyes and, though he could be on the quiet side, he was always observing life around him. When you got to know him, his wicked sense of humor emerged.

"I'm hoping to start it in about six weeks," Ty said. "I have to get those roofs fixed—and secure the funding for it—and I also want to pace myself. Plus, it will be nice when it's a little warmer out so we can do more outside without freezing."

"I get that." Wes leaned back, always easygoing. "Just make sure you don't plan it around the time of Braden and Lisa's wedding. It's only another month away."

"No, I wouldn't do that." Ty glanced over at his friend. "It seems like everyone is getting paired off here on the island—everyone but you."

Wes sliced his hand through the air, still maintaining his laid-back vibe. "No, not me. Not anytime soon."

"You sound pretty happy being single."

"I am."

"So was I—until I met Cassidy."

"And now you two are the poster couple for how to be happy and in love."

Ty chuckled. "I do feel blessed. I'm not going to lie."

"Women just make life complicated. Personally, I like making my own choices about what I'm going to do, how I'm going to spend my money, and what I'm going to eat."

"As long as you're happy." When the right one came along, his friend would change his mind.

Ty slowed his truck as they passed one of the large properties on the island. For years, the place had practically been a graveyard, but recently it had been brought back to the land of the living. He'd heard someone from out of town had bought it, but for the life of him, he couldn't figure out what was happening with the property now. A new campground? A mobile home community?

"You hear what's going on there?" Ty asked.

Wes followed Ty's gaze and frowned. "I heard some church bought it. They're doing revivals and retreats there or something. Not an especially friendly bunch."

"You've actually run into some of them?"

"I was on the ferry coming back this way from picking up some supplies a couple days ago. A woman had to get out of her car because she got seasick. I walked over to make sure she was okay. Anyway, I tried to make small talk. The only thing she told me was that she was coming here for a new start."

"The idea of starting over is very enticing for a lot of people," Ty said. Ty himself had come here because he'd taken vacations to the area as a child. His grandfather had left him the beach house, and he knew it would be the perfect place to start his nonprofit.

"Yeah, everyone who comes here seems to have secrets, don't they? Anyway, I left the conversation alone. I didn't want her to think I was hitting on her or something. She was in front of me as we exited the ferry, and I saw her pull up to the gate here."

"Interesting." Ty's foot hit the brakes softly as movement on the other side of the fence caught his eye.

A little girl ran to the iron slats and grabbed them, peering out at the road. A second later, a woman chased after her. Both wore khaki pants and some kind of beige tunic. The woman scolded the girl before grabbing her hand and pulling her away.

But, before the woman left, she glanced at Ty and Wes in the truck. She stared at them a moment, something deep yet hollow in her gaze. Finally, she scowled before turning her back and walking away.

"That was weird," Wes muttered.

His friend was right. Ty couldn't put his finger on exactly what was weird about the encounter, but the interaction just seemed off.

Live and let live, Ty. Live and let live.

But he was more curious now than ever about the new owners of that property.

That said, he had bigger things to be concerned about. Starting with that phone call about Cassidy's dad. There was more to the conversation than Cassidy had shared. In fact, he could see that the call had clearly shaken her.

And then there was the man he'd seen watching him and Cassidy earlier.

They'd been jogging, but Ty had spotted him in the distance, standing on the sand dune with his face turned toward them and sunglasses hiding his gaze.

Could he have been a fisherman? Someone on vacation?

Of course.

But another part of Ty feared the man had been sent here to find Cassidy. That he was affiliated with the deadly—yet supposedly disbanded—gang known as DH-7. Those in the gang wanted to make Cassidy pay after she'd killed their leader in self-defense while acting as an undercover cop.

Ty feared that Cassidy would never truly be safe.

And that was something he found hard to swallow.

———

CASSIDY CLIMBED into her SUV and took off toward the clinic, which was just down the road. Doc Clemson had called and asked her to come out. He said he had something to show her.

Lantern Beach Urgent Care Clinic was the only medical facility on the island. The practice wasn't set up for anything extensive, but it was sufficient for most emergencies in the community. Tucked away in a back corner of the building, near Doc Clemson's office, was the morgue—the area where the doc performed autopsies as well.

Cassidy called hello to the woman at the front desk before heading that way. The scent of antiseptic filled the air, but Cassidy was happy to see that the clinic looked empty.

Good. That meant there hadn't been any more tragedies here. For the time being, at least.

"Cassidy." Doc Clemson looked up from the cloth-draped body in front of him. "Or should I say, Chief Chambers."

"You know you can call me Cassidy." She stepped closer.

"I figured you'd be here quickly. I feel like I just put down my phone and now, boom! You're here. Told you you're giving Mac a run for his money for the title of best police chief Lantern Beach has ever seen." Clemson winked.

Cassidy grinned. "I don't think anyone will ever compare to Mac. Now, what did you want to show me?"

Doc Clemson's smile disappeared, and he glanced down at the body. "Well, for starters, I think you were right about the means of death. This man didn't drown —his lungs weren't filled with water."

Good to know.

"It appears he died of asphyxiation," Doc Clemson continued. "I'm guessing, based on bruising, that he had a rope around his neck. Maybe a noose."

"He hung himself?" Cassidy sucked in a quick breath.

"I don't know if he did it himself or if someone else did it to him. But the bruises around his neck clearly indicate that was the cause of death."

"If he hung himself, then how did he get into the ocean?" She mostly said the question to herself, though she was open to hearing any feedback Clemson might have.

"That's the question." Doc Clemson glanced at her, his look promising he was going to launch into something big. Leaving the sheet around the victim, Clemson rolled the man onto his side. "Take a look at this."

Cassidy crossed to the other side of the examination table to see what the doctor was talking about. She sucked in a breath when she saw the man's back—and the scars there.

Clemson's knowing look deepened. "That's what I thought too."

"What could these be from?" The marks were almost too numerous to count, but if Cassidy had to guess, she'd say there were twenty-five at least. Some were large, some were small. But it almost appeared …

"It looks like he was whipped with something, doesn't it?" Clemson asked, subtle grief in his gaze.

"Yeah, it sure does. How old do you think these are?"

"They've all scarred over, but they still retain a darker purple look to them. I'd guess our victim got these over the past six months."

"Someone was beating or torturing this man, Clemson."

He nodded grimly. "I know."

"Any idea *what* left those marks?"

He squinted as he glanced down at the man's back. "It's hard to say, but it's too thin to be a belt. My guess is that it's some kind of switch or whip."

Cassidy grabbed her phone and took a picture of the marks as another shiver went down her spine. "I don't like this."

"I don't either."

The thought that the person responsible for doing this to the victim might be on this island caused the blood in her veins to run cold.

Now more than ever, Cassidy needed to find out this man's identity.

CHAPTER THREE

After leaving the clinic, Cassidy pulled up in front of Mac MacArthur's place and paused. A grin curled her lip as she observed the scene there.

Mac had a group of about eight local kids—she assumed they were local, at least—out in his front yard. He'd set up what looked like a police training academy, and the kids were now navigating it while Mac appeared to keep time.

First, the kids ran through inflatable inner tubes, the colorful kind used to float around on in the water. They crawled under some volleyball nets that were flat and about a foot from the ground like a cargo net crawl at boot camp. They ended by grabbing water guns and hitting a target at the back of Mac's property.

All the while, Mac stood there with a stopwatch in his hands and a whistle near his mouth, yelling instructions to them. Mac, with his scrawny but strong build, his full head of white hair, his thin white beard and mustache ... he made being in your sixties look young.

Mac was one of Cassidy's favorite people ever. He was the town's former longtime police chief, and the man always had a mischievous glint in his eyes. But he was also dependable and capable.

He'd been helping Cassidy by filling in at the police department whenever he could. She desperately needed to hire someone else, especially before the busy summer season began. Finding good help was harder than she'd imagined, though.

When Mac saw her approaching, he blew his whistle and told everyone to take a five-minute water break. The kids ran toward a table at the back of Mac's property. He owned a small cottage here—probably less than nine hundred square feet—with cedar siding and built on stilts, like most of the homes in this area. He was about a block off the beach, only because he'd bought this before property close to the ocean tripled in price two decades ago.

Cassidy knew that only because people in town liked to talk about the changes to the former fishing community. Many of the locals—and they were the ones who stayed around in the winter with nothing but time on their hands—had lived through decades of changes in the area.

Mac was just one of the reasons she loved this place.

Cassidy thought of the phone call she'd gotten from her mother. Her dad ... while she hadn't been especially close with him, her heart still ached at the thought of what he was going through. He'd always been strong and smart and capable.

Being sidelined like this ... it would be devastating for him. And for Cassidy's mom. Appearance was everything to her family, and the golden couple now had to face this medical event.

It would be the test of her parents' relationship.

Her thoughts shifted to her mom's proposal. Leave Lantern Beach? No, it wasn't a possibility. She'd gained her life here, her life away from the pressures of having a dominant, high-profile family. Of fighting her way past the expectations society had on her. She'd become her own person.

She and Ty didn't have much—but they didn't need much, as long as they had each other ... and Kujo. Sure, money was tight sometimes. Trying to make the nonprofit work could be a struggle. But there was nowhere else she'd rather be.

Home is the place where your heart is happy. The wisdom came from a Day-at-a-Glance calendar that had once belonged to her best friend Lucy. Cassidy had practically memorized the advice there, and it seemed to serve her well at the most appropriate of times.

She shifted her thoughts back to her reason for coming to see Mac.

"What's going on here?" Cassidy paused on the prickly grass at the front of Mac's house and watched participants gulp down cups of water from an orange cooler. The mid-morning sun tried to warm her face, but the winter wind wouldn't let it. At least the kids were probably warm as they spent their energy out here.

"I'm doing a boot camp and trying to train some kids on the basics of law enforcement while they're young. I've been doing it during the island's spring break for the past ten years." His gaze remained on his kids, like an ever-vigilant watchman.

"I'm surprised we don't have more recruits then," Cassidy said. "Hardly anyone on the actual island has applied."

"After everything that's happened here over the past nine months, they're too scared."

"Can't really blame them for that." Drug busts, human trafficking, gang members, dead bodies … the place had exploded with crime, it seemed.

Or maybe it was Mac's boot camp that had scared potential applicants away. If Cassidy had to guess, this spring break training was no joke.

As the kids yelled and laughed in the distance, Mac stole a glance at her. "You found anyone else to hire yet?"

Former police chief Alan Bozeman had left at the end of the summer. Two of his officers had stuck around, but one had taken another job down in South Carolina three months ago, leaving Cassidy with only one other officer.

"As a matter of fact, we have an interview tomorrow with some guy from Ohio," Cassidy said.

"Did you vet him?"

Cassidy raised her eyebrows. "Did I vet him? Can

Mac MacArthur say the alphabet forward, backward, forward and backward while skipping every other letter?"

The man had some unusual talents—that being one of them.

"I knew you would have." He grinned like a proud papa. "This is one of your first real interviews, isn't it?"

"It is. No one else really struck me as ready for this job, so why waste people's time?"

"Agreed." He narrowed his eyes at the kids in the distance. "Bobby, that water gun is not a flirtation device. Stop shooting Suzy and put it down!"

Cassidy hid a smile.

Mac turned back to her. "Sorry about that. Anyway, what about this summer? Did the mayor agree to let you hire a couple more officers in the summer?"

"He did. I'm hoping Braden will be one of them. His therapy—and Lisa—has been working wonders for him. But I do need his doctor's approval before that's definite."

Braden Dillinger was one of Ty's old friends. He had PTSD and some brain injuries he was working through. Once he was cleared, he'd make a great cop.

Mac studied her face. "I take it you didn't come this way to tell me all that."

The grim reality of today's events pressed on her chest. "I didn't. You heard about the body on the beach?"

"You know it. If I didn't have this boot camp, I would have been there like a thorn in your side."

"You're never a thorn in my side. But I would like your advice on something."

"I've got advice like a dog has fleas. Shoot."

"I'm trying to identify our victim. I believe he was murdered. And I believe he was abused in some way beginning about six months ago. He has scars …"

"Sad yet intriguing. Go on."

Cassidy chewed on her bottom lip for a moment. "Should I put out a press release to find his identity? It's going to bring Lantern Beach into the spotlight—and I'm not sure that's the kind of spotlight we want."

Mac frowned and squinted. "I see where you're coming from. You probably don't want to be the one whose face is on the news doing a press conference of some type."

"Exactly." No, the fact that Cassidy was here needed to remain a secret. There were still men out there who would kill her if they realized she was alive.

She'd taken on a new name. Changed her hair. Gotten married. Those were all safeguards, but they weren't foolproof.

"Run this guy's details through NamUs. See if there are any matches. If that doesn't get you anywhere, then you're going to need to appeal to the media. The last thing you want is for people here to think you're keeping secrets. It will build distrust, and you don't want that, especially after that last wahoo we had in your position."

Chief Alan Bozeman—or Bozoman, as Mac had

called him—had been a disgrace to the profession. Thankfully, he was long gone now.

"That's what I thought. I just needed someone older and wiser to run it past." Being a detective in Seattle was totally different than being in charge of a small police department. At times, Cassidy missed having superiors who were more experienced to turn to for advice.

It was one more reason she was thankful for Mac.

"Don't know about the wiser part, but definitely an old geezer."

Cassidy squeezed his arm affectionately before taking a step back. "You'll never be a geezer, Mac. But you'll always be a friend."

As she turned to head back to her car—amidst Mac blowing his whistle and calling his boot camp recruits back over—she froze.

That feeling washed over her again. That feeling of being watched.

Yet, as Cassidy looked around, she saw no one.

Was she just being paranoid? Or had DH-7 found her again? Even worse, could DH-7 look like someone she knew and trusted?

———

BACK AT THE STATION, Cassidy typed all the victim's information into NamUs but got no matches. NamUs, the National Missing and Unidentified Persons System, was a database and resource center for missing people across the United States.

Cassidy leaned back into her office chair and let out a sigh.

So far today, she only had questions and no answers.

She ran a hand over her face. Speaking of today, it had been a long one. Too long—and it was only two in the afternoon.

Cassidy knew when she'd taken over here on Lantern Beach that the island wasn't all small-town goodness. No, most people came here to get away from something. Sometimes it was a busy work schedule, but other times it was problems, heartaches … sometimes even danger.

Cassidy had been a detective in Seattle until an undercover assignment had forced her into hiding. Cassidy wasn't even her real name, and only two people on the island knew that—Ty and Mac. They were the only ones who could ever know.

Yes, she knew all about people coming here to get away from something.

She just never thought she'd end up staying. That she'd end up falling in love with both the island and with Ty. That the community would draw her in like a long-lost family. That the sandy shores would beckon a peace like she'd never known.

Now she couldn't ever imagine leaving. It didn't matter that she'd left a life where she'd wanted for nothing. Her dad was a tech mogul who had more money than some small countries. But money didn't equate with happiness. Cassidy knew that firsthand.

Casting those thoughts aside to focus on the present, Cassidy turned to look at the board she'd created beside her desk. There in the center of the board was a glossy picture of the man who'd washed up on the beach.

"Who are you?" she muttered, staring at the image of his lifeless face.

Though it was hard to imagine while looking at the grotesque photo, he'd once been a living, breathing person. But, in death, his face was swollen. His body had begun to decay. But his eyes—closed in the photo— had once contained life. They'd once been windows to the man's soul. Those eyes had seen things that had shaped him into the person he'd ended up being before death had claimed him.

What happened to you? How did you get those scars?

Everyone deserved closure. Even people who were nameless. People who hadn't been reported missing. People who seemed forgotten.

The forgotten deserved justice also.

Which was why Cassidy was going to have to release this information to the media. She hoped she could keep herself out of it. The last thing she needed was her face plastered on TVs, the Internet, or in newspapers across the country.

No, she had to stay low-key. She had no other choice.

She looked through the other photos that had been taken, searching for anything she might have missed earlier. She'd printed them off in the office so she could add them to the board that contained all the information on the case. Right now, the glossy photos slid across her fingertips.

She paused when she saw the man's legs. Not his legs specifically. No, his jeans.

There were dirt stains on the knees.

Just like the man Cassidy had seen on the beach earlier. The one who'd been standing off on the sand dune in the distance. The one who'd scurried when she walked his way.

The first spike of satisfaction raced through her.

Maybe this was her first real clue.

It had to be.

But until she could figure out how the men were connected, she would have to do what she could. She began penning her press release.

Unidentified male. Approximately 35 years old. 185 pounds. 5'11".

CHAPTER FOUR

Ty waited outside The Crazy Chefette for Cassidy.

The restaurant—an old Coast Guard building—was now painted yellow with cheerful pink shutters. A large sign with the restaurant's name also featured a cartoonish woman wearing a lab coat and holding a beaker in one hand and a spatula in the other. The words under the name read "mad food created by a crazy woman."

Lisa Garth wasn't crazy, but she *had* been a scientist. In a way, she still was, only her experiments now involved food instead of chemicals. No one ever knew exactly what they were going to get when they saw the menu here.

Lisa had invited the gang over to her restaurant to have dinner together. They tried to meet at least once a week to hang out and have Bible study as well. The routine kept them all connected.

The eatery was closed except for weekends—at least

for another month or so. Many businesses in the area shut down in the slow winter season. There weren't enough customers to justify the expenses of staying open.

Cassidy parked at the side of the building, climbed out, and walked toward Ty, wearing her official police uniform and jacket. Ty had seen her in the outfit hundreds of times already, but he still felt a rush of pride when he realized just how far Cassidy had come in the past several months.

She'd gone from a big-city detective and rich girl with a bounty on her head to a capable law enforcement officer who enjoyed the simple things in life.

And she looked good. Then again, Cassidy could wear sackcloth and look good.

He kissed Cassidy's cheek as she stopped in front of him. "Hey, gorgeous."

"Hey, yourself. How's it going?"

Something about the way she said the words made Ty realize that they had unfinished conversations. He needed to talk to her more about that phone call with her mom this morning. And he needed to mention the man he'd seen watching them.

But this just didn't seem like the time.

He remembered Cassidy's question and shrugged, quickly thinking through his day. "I can't complain too much about my day. But you, on the other hand, look tired."

There were small circles beneath her eyes, and her gaze wasn't as bright as usual.

She frowned and raked a hand through her blonde hair—the parts of it that weren't pulled back into a bun, at least. "Just finished a lot of the nonglamorous side of police work. Paperwork, primarily. I also penned the press release so we can try to identify this guy."

"No leads, huh?"

She shook her head, but something lingered in the back of her gaze ... something that was bothering her, if Ty had to guess.

"No. But he had these scars on his back... Ty, I don't know what happened to the man, but I think he might have been tortured." She said the words softly, with obvious respect for both the dead and for those who'd suffered.

Ty sucked in a breath, a million memories pummeling him. Memories of his time in the Middle East. Memories of his comrades in arms and the things they'd gone through at the hands of evil men.

There were some things a man would never forget—and images of finding one of his men after he'd been tortured was one of them.

"That doesn't sound good." Ty's words were an understatement, to say the least. But he didn't want to overreact.

Though no dead body was run-of-the-mill, he hadn't expected that news. He didn't like the bad feeling it left in his gut—especially since Cassidy would be investigating. There were killers who acted in the heat of the moment, and then there were killers who acted after premeditated planning—people who liked to see others suffer.

Those people were the ones who scared him the most.

And the thought of Cassidy investigating someone like that … it caused his heart to twist with protectiveness.

Cassidy slipped into his shadow, squinting against the setting sun behind him. "There's a chance he could have washed up from somewhere other than Lantern Beach. Maybe up north from the Outer Banks? Maybe even down south from Myrtle Beach. We're checking with the Coast Guard to find out the pattern of the ocean current recently."

"You're just starting with this investigation," Ty told her. "I'm sure things will begin coming together."

"I wish I felt that certain. I know we'll eventually find some answers. I just don't know that I'm going to like any of them."

"If this guy was tortured …" Ty started. He couldn't stop thinking about what Cassidy had told him.

"What?" Cassidy stepped closer and studied his expression.

He swung his head back and forth as images pounded his thoughts. "I don't know. That makes this case even more high stakes. I don't want …"

Cassidy squeezed his arm reassuringly. "I'll be careful, Ty. I promise."

After a moment of hesitation, he nodded. "I know."

Just then, Lisa stuck her head out the front door. Her

blonde hair swished across her shoulders, and her expressive eyes were wide and clearly trying to communicate ... something.

"Ty. Cassidy. Thank goodness you're here."

Cassidy narrowed her eyes and stepped back, their conversation obviously done for now. "What's going on, Lisa?"

Lisa's normally cheerful face looked pale and stiff. "You didn't hear?"

"Hear what?" Ty glanced at Cassidy and saw that her face reflected his own confusion.

Lisa glanced around like someone might be watching before motioning for them to come inside. "Follow me."

They trailed her into the restaurant. The scent of savory meat and onions filled the air, but Ty had no time to appreciate it. Lisa hurried through the kitchen and to the back where the walk-in freezer was.

Lisa threw them one more look before opening the door and pointing inside.

Ty squinted as he peered into the space. Was that ...

"It's not what you think." Lisa's words shot out rapidly and sounded laced with anxiety.

Ty twisted his head, trying to think of what else it might be besides ... "It looks like a dead body on a stretcher."

Lisa frowned. "Okay, it is what it looks like. But not the way you think."

Ty glanced around, only half joking as he asked, "Is Braden okay?"

"That's not Braden!" Lisa's eyes were as wide as her sausage balls. "Braden had to run to the grocery store for me real fast. Who do you think I am?"

"I was just kidding."

Cassidy took a step closer to the figure, her voice professional and reasoned. "Who's in the body bag?"

"Doc Clemson didn't tell you?" Lisa's eyes remained wide and slightly frantic.

"Tell me what?"

"The freezer at the morgue died," Lisa said. "Doc Clemson asked me if he could keep this ... this ... dead person here! In my freezer!"

Ty sucked in a quick breath, halfway horrified and halfway amused. "Wow."

"He didn't tell me." Cassidy frowned at the stretcher.

That was definitely a body bag, right in the middle of her shelves full of frozen produce and meat.

"What if my customers hear about this?" Lisa threw her hands in the air, her eyes almost comically wide as she began to pace. "They'll never want to eat here again."

"I'm sure that's not true," Cassidy said. "Besides, we won't tell anyone."

"What about Leggott? Or Doc Clemson? They delivered this body bag. Anyone could have driven past and seen it."

"You could have said no, right?" Ty asked.

"This is Doc Clemson. I have to keep him on my

good side. I never know when I might need him, and he's the only doctor here on the island."

"Good point." Ty glanced at Cassidy. "You didn't know about this?"

"No, the body is in Doc's custody. He didn't have to run it by me. He must have seen Leggott and asked him to help."

"It sounded like it was rather sudden," Lisa added before her lips pulled downward in an all-encompassing frown. "What am I going to do?"

"Nothing," Cassidy said. "We'll just pretend like this never happened."

———

AN HOUR LATER, Cassidy and her group of island friends were all seated at some tables that had been pushed together in the center of the restaurant. They chatted as they ate the food Lisa had prepared—hot beef sundaes. The recipe was surprisingly good with roast beef on the bottom, a scoop of mashed potatoes in the middle, gravy drizzled across everything, and a cherry tomato on top.

Cassidy and Ty sat beside each other. Lisa and her fiancé, Braden, sat across from them. Rounding out their group of friends were Austin Brooks and Skye Lavinia, who were also dating; Wes—Mr. Single Forever and Proud of It; and Pastor Jack Wilson and his new bride, Juliette.

Cassidy glanced down the table at all her friends

and smiled. No one here was perfect, but they'd also made a pact that no one stood alone. Knowing she had a support system girding her meant the world to Cassidy.

"Jack and Juliette look happy, don't they?" Ty whispered, his breath tickling her ear.

She glanced at them as they giggled together at some kind of inside joke. "Yeah, they really do. They just fit. I was skeptical about their quick marriage, but they look like they were made for each other, just like the ocean and the sand."

All her friends here seemed to be getting paired off, and Cassidy couldn't be happier for them. She wanted all her friends to experience the over-the-moon joy she'd found since marrying Ty.

Just then, Wes stood and started toward the kitchen.

"Wait!" Lisa lurched to her feet. "Where are you going?"

"Just to grab some more ice." He held up his cup, looking confused.

"I'll get it." Lisa reached him and tried to snatch the cup from his hand.

Wes stared at her, his confusion even more pronounced as his eyebrows shoved together and his eyes narrowed. He pulled his cup toward him, almost protectively, but no doubt to aggravate Lisa as well. "I don't mind."

In the blink of an eye, Lisa had grabbed the cup from him. "Neither do I. It's my restaurant. I win. Have a seat. I insist."

Wes raised his hands in exaggerated defeat. "Okay … I was just trying to be helpful."

Cassidy and Ty exchanged a smile. Lisa obviously didn't want to risk Wes discovering the body in the freezer. If Wes *did* find out, he'd never let her live it down. He was like a big brother with his teasing sometimes.

Cassidy hated to cut into the otherwise lighthearted conversation, but a question pressed in on her. As soon as Lisa had returned with Wes's drink and there was a pause in the conversation, Cassidy cleared her throat.

"Anyone heard any town scuttlebutt about the dead body that washed ashore?" she asked.

No one blinked an eye at her question. The local crime beat was part of their normal conversation. Here on the island, it was a part of most people's normal conversations.

"Someone in the grocery store was saying they thought he was a fisherman who fell out of his boat a few weeks ago," Braden said.

Nope, he didn't match the description. Cassidy had checked.

"I heard my neighbors saying they thought he was a windsurfer from Hatteras," Skye added.

Nope, Cassidy had checked that also. "They already found that guy—he was alive."

"Several years ago, someone fell off a cruise ship out in the Atlantic and washed up here," Wes said.

"I suppose stranger things have happened, but that theory isn't even on our radar right now," Cassidy said.

Pastor Jack raised his hand down at the end. "I haven't heard any theories. But have you ever considered that maybe he's one of the new people who have moved into that old campground near town?"

That was an interesting question. "No, I haven't considered that. Do you know anything about the people who have moved there?"

Cassidy had been curious about the group, but finding out any information on them seemed impossible. They kept to themselves and hardly ever left the gated community. Even Cassidy, as an officer of the law, had trouble discovering any details on the crowd.

"Every time I go past, I think of Waco," Austin said. "And I'm not talking about *Fixer Upper*. I'm talking about David Koresh."

"You think it's a cult there?" Ty asked.

"I don't know if it's a cult, but I think it's weird. Really weird." Austin shook his head, his eyebrows raised and a doubtful look on his face. "Everyone kind of dresses the same. They keep their heads down. Once they go in, they don't come out. You put the pieces together."

Cassidy let his words sink in.

A cult? It seemed far-fetched, but what if he was onto something?

It was definitely a theory she wanted to keep in mind.

CHAPTER FIVE

In the middle of a rousing conversation about the best fishing holes on the island, Cassidy's phone rang yet again. It was never-ending today. This time, it was Carter Denver, the island's local singer/songwriter.

"Hey, Chief," he started.

"Hey." Cassidy stepped away from the rest of her friends as their voices rose in a good-natured debate. "I have a feeling you're not calling about providing entertainment therapy to people at the police department."

He chuckled. "No, not quite. I wish I was calling for a simple reason. But there's something I think you ought to see."

Again. What could it possibly be now? "Sure thing. Are you out at your place?"

"I am."

"I'll be right there."

Ty went with her to Carter's apartment. He lived above a shop in the boardwalk area of the town.

Cassidy had stopped by once before with Ty, and Carter had cooked them dinner. He was an extremely talented yet nice, all-around guy—but he was also one who didn't open up a lot about his past and what had brought him to this island. He could easily be making a living off his music somewhere else.

Cassidy figured he would share his story when he was ready.

Carter met them at the door before they even knocked, his German shepherd standing happily beside him, tongue stretched nearly to the ground.

"Thanks for coming," he said. "Come on in."

They stepped inside and listened to the soothing strands of acoustic music floating from a speaker somewhere in the distance. The whole place had an artistic touch with unique paintings, rich colors on the walls, and knickknacks from his travels.

"So, Bo got out today and went for a little traipse through town," Carter started, looking down at his dog and giving him a stern look. "He likes to do that sometimes, and he's been seen all the way down at the docks before. But he always comes back, thank goodness."

"That's good. He's a curious guy, huh?" Cassidy patted the dog's head.

"He is … but he brought me back a present today."

"What's that?" Cassidy asked.

Carter frowned, walked into the kitchen, and presented them with a paper bag. "I'll let you see for yourself."

The last time someone had said that to Cassidy, Clemson had shown her scars all over John Doe's back.

After a moment of hesitation, she opened the bag. She squinted when she saw what was inside. "A bone?"

Carter nodded, still looking tentative. "I'm no expert on these things, but I don't think that's any ordinary bone."

Cassidy and Ty exchanged a glance.

"That's what I'm afraid of," Cassidy muttered, reaching for a plastic bag on the counter. "You mind?"

"Not at all."

Using the disposable plastic as a shield, she reached into the grocery bag and lifted the bone out. It was four inches long with a two-inch ball at one end. The shaft was about one inch. Human? It could be. But she was no expert on bones.

"I'm going to have to let Doc Clemson look at this," she said. "I don't suppose you have any idea where Bo found it?"

"No idea. It could have been anywhere. I will tell you that he's a bit muddier than usual."

Mud … Cassidy remembered the mud on the jeans of the man who'd been standing on the dune. Could this be connected? It was too early to tell. But she kept that possibility in the back of her mind.

———

CASSIDY DROPPED the bone with Clemson, who wasn't able to definitively ID it either. Instead, he would send it off to the state lab. But he suspected that the bone could indeed be human, and Bo could have dug up an old grave on the island. They wouldn't proceed until they knew something for sure. Clemson said it could take several days to get test results.

Back at home, Cassidy cuddled up on the couch beside Ty, her favorite drink in hand. She wanted nothing more than to relax, but she couldn't. She had too much on her mind.

With Kujo sitting at her feet and Ty beside her on the couch, she jolted up, instantly missing Ty's warmth.

She gripped the glass in her hands and looked over at her husband. "I didn't have a chance to tell you about the phone call with my mother yet. Not all of it, at least."

"You told me your dad had a stroke and wasn't doing well."

She rubbed her lips together, still trying to comprehend all the implications of their conversation. "That's part of it. The other part is that she wants me to move back to Seattle and take over the company."

Ty straightened. "What? How could she even ask that? She knows what happened."

"I know. But she insists that I could get security to keep me safe."

"I wish that were true, but … the limelight is the last place you need to be. Besides, I've never heard you mention taking over your dad's company. Was that ever on your radar, even?"

Cassidy shook her head. "No, it wasn't. But my dad

has always wanted to keep the business in the family. That's why he was so disappointed when I became a cop instead. But I think, deep inside, he figured I'd come back around."

Ty shook his head, his eyes narrowed with thought. "Your mom was serious?"

"Yes, she was serious. She doesn't want word to leak about my dad until they have a plan in place."

"She's risking an awful lot just for a company."

"Alpha Tech sounds like just a company to a lot of people, but, to my mom and dad, it was their other baby. It was the thing they nurtured. That always did just as they wanted. That exceeded their expectations and made them proud."

Unlike me, Cassidy thought silently. She'd always had a mind of her own, and her parents hadn't been able to control her as they did everything else in their lives.

Ty squeezed her knee. "I know you and your parents had a strained relationship. I'm sorry they're putting this pressure on you now. It's not fair. They're asking you to put your life on the line for their business."

"I'm sure they don't see it that way. They're the type who don't see problems. They only look for solutions. And, in their minds, money can buy anything— including safety."

"They obviously don't realize the power of DH-7."

"No, their realm is more corporate spies or global hackers. It's a different kind of dangerous."

"Their ideas and finances are the only things in danger from those crimes."

"Exactly." She crossed her arms across her chest.

"Hey." Ty nudged her. "It's going to be okay."

The truth was, how could Cassidy be the person everyone needed her to be? The town needed her to keep law and order. But the hours she had to put in to do that meant less time with Ty. And that meant she wasn't always there for him like she wanted to be. And now her parents supposedly needed her.

Though she'd learned not to be defined by other people's expectations of her, the thought of failing the people she cared about caused an unseen weight to press down on her.

"You don't regret staying here, do you?" Ty asked.

His words caused an ache to form in her chest. "What? No. Never."

He pulled her into a warm hug, his arms enveloping her completely. "Good. Because I don't ever want to hold you back. I don't want to lose you, either."

"You're never going to lose me, Ty. And you're not holding me back. The life my parents have isn't the kind of life I ever wanted for myself."

Ty kissed the top of her head. "Good."

She settled her head on his chest and listened to the steady thumping beneath her ear. She'd meant the words. Lantern Beach with Ty was the only place for her.

But that didn't stop the tension from pulling inside her.

CHAPTER SIX

Moriah felt an unusual amount of jitters as she stepped out of her trailer.

A brisk morning wind swept over the water and hit her exposed skin.

Thou must suffer for the sake of the cause.

All her clothes had been given to charity—including her coat.

The cause was worth the sacrifice.

It felt good to believe in something. To be a part of a group.

Everyone had welcomed her last night and, for the first time in forever, Moriah had truly felt like she belonged.

First, a nice woman named Elizabeth—a woman a few years older than Moriah who would be her mentor —had given her a tour. There were forty campers and trailers here at the compound. In the center was the Meeting Place. Inside, it was nothing fancy, but Gilead wanted to make it more presentable—a place with worthy workmanship, he'd said.

It made sense. Give your best to God. Giving your best meant not settling for shabby workmanship.

Gilead and his advisors met in the room above the Meeting Place. She wasn't sure, but Gilead might live up there also.

There were also gardens. Even though it was winter, they still needed to be tended for the winter crop. And a greenhouse provided protection from the elements for other plants as Gilead's Cove tried to become a self-sustaining community.

Everyone here had a job. Today Moriah would find out what hers was. Maybe she could cook. She'd always loved cooking. Or childcare. She'd always loved children as well.

That was what she would end up doing. She felt sure of it.

Everything here felt so right, and her instincts told her that she was where she should be. Certainly, things would continue to fall into place and fulfillment would be a part of her future. Gilead had promised her that much.

Her feet, clad in sandals, hit the rocky yet sandy soil. She joined the others on the path that led toward the Meeting Place. No one said anything. She'd been instructed not to speak before morning prayers.

She held her head down. It was important, she'd been told. A sign of humility.

And humility was where change could begin.

She desperately needed this to work. It was her last hope, so she needed to do whatever was necessary to ensure she found her place. If being here didn't work to change her life then nothing would. She'd have to admit defeat—to admit that she'd failed at life.

And she might as well end it all.

She stepped into the Meeting Place, and relief instantly filled her, from her skin all the way to her bones. It wasn't warm in here—but it wasn't cold either. At least the walls protected her from the cool breeze that raked across the island.

She followed the example of everyone else as they gathered in a circle at the center of the Meeting Place. Tables and wooden chairs had been set up in the room, in front of a rickety-looking stage. The room was dark. At one time, there might have been windows, but they'd been boarded up. Certainly there were less distractions if people couldn't see outside.

When everyone had arrived, they prayed together and then ate breakfast in silence—another ritual. Afterward, the tables were put away, the chairs were set facing the stage, and Gilead stepped out.

The way Moriah's heart pounded, he might as well be a celebrity stepping out for autographs. The man was a star.

He began a motivational talk, encouraging everyone to live up to their potential.

Potential.

That was what she'd focus on. Potential and purpose.

As the meeting ended, Gilead handed out instructions for the day.

Moriah waited eagerly to learn what her role would be.

Dietrich, one of Gilead's assistants, stopped in front of her and glanced at a clipboard. "Moriah Roberts, your assigned duty today is to clean the bathrooms in the trailers."

She sucked in a breath. Bathrooms. She'd always hated cleaning bathrooms. Why wouldn't she be assigned something in her gifting? She'd done an assessment test yesterday. And—

"Moriah," Dietrich repeated.

She glanced up and nodded. "Yes, thank you."

"Thank you, sir," he corrected.

"Thank you, sir."

"And …"

That's right. There was something else she was supposed to say. What was it? Her thoughts muddled as insecurity gripped her. The kids at school had always teased her, saying she was stupid. She'd overheard one of her teachers telling her mom that she'd probably never graduate from high school.

Those words had been burned into her brain, and for a long time, she'd let them dictate her future. But not anymore. She couldn't believe the lies that she'd held about herself for so long.

"Thank you, sir. And with gladness I will go forth and serve." That was it.

That seemed to appease Dietrich, and he moved on to the next person.

This would just take some getting used to. That didn't mean there was anything wrong with the way things were done here. It just meant it was different.

She needed to be open-minded.

Her only regret was that she'd left her parents behind. Her poor parents. Her dad had been having heart problems, and her mom looked on the verge of a mental breakdown. They'd been so wrapped up in their own problems that they'd hardly noticed any of Moriah's problems.

Moriah knew they loved her. But even their love hadn't been enough to make her feel accepted.

CHAPTER SEVEN

"No, Mrs. Jones," Cassidy said into the phone the next morning. "I assure you the body that washed ashore wasn't your husband, Frank. I just saw him this morning at the general store. What's that? You were hoping it was him? You know, Pastor Jack at the community church meets with couples for counseling to help work through feelings like this …"

A few minutes later, Cassidy ended the call and sighed. Ever since she'd released the information to the media, she'd been vetting calls—all of which had been a waste of time. Someone thought it was an old boyfriend from California. Another thought John Doe was someone they'd seen on a missing-persons poster. Mrs. Jones hoped it was her husband.

Her phone buzzed, and Cassidy almost didn't want to respond. But it was Melva, and the woman would just knock at her door if Cassidy didn't pick up.

"Chief, we have a call on line two," Melva said. "A woman says she knows who John Doe is."

Exhaustion pressed on Cassidy. She had to take these calls, even if they were a waste of time. All she needed was one person who actually had relevant information to make this worth it.

"Put her through," she said, but her voice lacked enthusiasm.

A moment later, Cassidy spoke with someone named Trisha Hartman from West Virginia.

"I … I saw the news about an unidentified body that had washed up, and I may know who it is," the woman started, her voice shaky.

"I'm listening." Cassidy grabbed a pen and piece of paper, ready to jot down notes, just in case.

"I think … I think he might be my estranged husband. His name was—is—I don't know how to say it. Anyway, Al Hartman … I think. The picture … it was hard to make out all the details, but there was a resemblance, you know?"

Al Hartman, Cassidy wrote. "You're doing just fine, Ms. Hartman. When was the last time you saw Al?"

"It's probably been seven months. It was around September, when school was starting, actually. I really thought he'd pop into our lives over the holidays, but he didn't. We have two children. Sylvie is ten, and Lucas is twelve."

Cassidy scribbled some more notes. "Did anything in particular happen the last time you spoke?"

"No, not really. Al sounded upbeat. He told me he'd

found a new lease on life and that he was going away to start again."

A new lease on life? What had signaled that reaction? Revelations like that usually didn't come out of the blue.

And then there was the practical … "What about child support?"

"He sold everything in his name. It wasn't much, but it netted him around forty thousand dollars. He had some antique cars he'd restored. Anyway, he gave the money all to me. Said he didn't need it anymore."

"Was that unusual?" Cassidy needed to know if he was the spontaneous type of guy or if this was totally out of character. Because most people didn't easily hand over that amount of money during a contentious split.

"Totally unusual. He liked his stuff—too much. He liked his stuff more than he liked me, for that matter." Trisha let out a bitter laugh. "That was one of the many reasons we separated."

Cassidy closed the door to her office as some tourists clattered into the building to ask for directions. That wasn't all that unusual here in Lantern Beach. People came in to ask for restaurant recommendations, and once had asked for sunburn advice. The station was like the town visitor center at times.

She sat back down in her chair. "What caused the change of heart? Any idea?"

"Al started going to this group for people with depression. He met some people there, and they started taking him to these meetings … they were like church."

Cassidy's spine straightened as curiosity tingled inside her. "What do you mean 'like church'?"

"I mean, they believed Jesus was just a prophet, but the true son of God was still coming. Or he'd just come. Or some other nonsense. I didn't ask many questions. After all, Al seemed a lot happier, so I figured it wasn't hurting anything."

"He seemed happy enough to sell all his possessions, apparently." The extreme life changes sounded warning bells in Cassidy's head. Dramatic shifts in lifestyle called for a deeper examination, in Cassidy's experience.

"Yes, his changes were dramatic enough that he decided to move away from his kids. To pretend like they didn't exist anymore." More bitterness edged into Trisha's voice.

"Was that surprising? Did he have a good relationship with them?" Cassidy would circle back around to this religious group in a moment.

"It was very surprising. He loved—loves—his kids. They were almost like another one of his possessions, you know? His trophies. When I left him … he went downhill. Fast. He begged me to stay with him. Said he would change. I said I had to see him change first."

An ultimatum. Selling his possessions. New friends. Cassidy continued to take notes. "Were there any other changes in his life that you're aware of?"

"Yeah, he lost his job. That only made his depression worse."

"Where did he work?"

"He was an engineer for a textile plant up here. I guess he started making stupid mistakes, and his boss thought he was unreliable. That only added to his mental state. It was like a circle that kept spiraling, you know?"

"Yeah, I can imagine." Cassidy paused. "Ms. Hartman, we're going to need someone to come in and ID the body."

"That's ... that's what I thought. My mom said she could keep the kids for me. I can leave tomorrow."

"That would be great. In the meantime, is there anything distinguishing about Al that might help us ID him before you arrive?"

Trisha paused for a minute. "He has a birthmark behind his ear. It's a red oval. About half-an-inch long. And he should have a scar from where he had his appendix removed."

Cassidy would need to check that—which meant she'd need to go to Lisa's sometime today. "How about his back? Were there any scars there?"

"His back?" Her voice rang with surprise. "What kind of scars? No, I don't think so."

Cassidy didn't want to share the details, not since it was an open investigation and not until she knew for sure this was the right guy. "Just asking. Ms. Hartman, could you email me a picture of Al?"

"Of course. I'm not at home right now, but I'll send it when I am. Give me a couple hours."

"One more question," Cassidy said. "Did this religious group have a name? Or was there anything note-worthy about them?"

"Not that I know of. I didn't really pay much attention. Now I wish that I had."

Cassidy rattled off an email address before saying, "Thank you for calling. I'll see you sometime tomorrow, and I can put you through to Melva if you need some help planning how to get here."

It sounded like Al could be their guy.

But the bad feeling in Cassidy's gut coiled like a viper poising to strike.

Al had a spiritual awakening? He sold everything and left everyone behind?

That sounded either like he'd had a come-to-Jesus moment and radically transformed his life ... or he'd joined a cult.

And when Cassidy thought about a cult, she thought about the group that had moved in at the gated property here on the island. Were they a cult? She didn't know. But it was time to find out. And she would start by visiting and seeing if anyone there could identify their John Doe.

It was worth a shot.

But first she needed to see John Doe's body again.

———

TWO OTHER PHONE calls revealed that Lisa had left the island, looking for a wedding dress up in Nags Head and that Doc Clemson was in the middle of surgery and couldn't speak. When Lisa returned this evening, Cassidy would stop by to look at the body again.

Until then, Cassidy would continue her investigation. She pulled her police SUV up to the gate of the old campground.

From what she'd gathered, this used to be called Henderson's RV Resort. Apparently, management had gone downhill and prices had gone up. Eventually, the property went into foreclosure and had become an eyesore on the island. People had been relieved when it finally sold, hoping the new owner would fix the place up.

A small, metal box at the guard station seemed to be Cassidy's only hope of getting inside this place. Otherwise, she'd have to breach an iron fence. She pressed the button there and waited.

When no one answered after five seconds, Cassidy pressed the button again. Finally, static came across the line, and a distant voice said, "Can I help you?"

"Police Chief Cassidy Chambers here," she started. "I'd like to talk to someone inside about a possible crime."

"One moment."

Cassidy tapped her fingers against her steering wheel as she waited for someone to return to the line. They had no obligation to let her in—not without a search warrant. But she really hoped they would.

Just when she thought she would have to turn around and leave, a man meandered toward the gate.

He wore dirty khakis and a white tunic. She'd guess him to be in his forties. He had thinning red hair and an angular face.

After climbing into the guard station, he slid the window open and leaned toward her. "I'm Barnabas. How can I help you?"

"Hi, Barnabas." She flashed her badge and watched as the man blanched. She got that reaction a lot.

"We don't usually take visitors here." His voice quivered ever so slightly.

"I'm not really a visitor," Cassidy said. "I'm the police chief here on the island."

"Yes, we understand that. But this is a place of peace and tranquility. We've worked hard to establish that and don't want anything to mess it up."

"I promise to be as peaceful as possible. I'm just asking questions about a body that washed up here on the island."

"We don't want trouble."

"Neither do I."

Finally, he nodded. "Okay, then. You can come in. But you'll need to leave your vehicle here and go the rest of the way by foot. Like I said, this is a place of peace."

"Sure thing."

Cassidy followed his directions and parked her vehicle right inside the gate. As she trailed Barnabas down what used to be a gravel road that led to the campground, her arm brushed the holstered gun at her waist. She found a strange comfort in knowing it was there in case she needed it.

Her eyes scanned everything around her—the RVs, the gravel road, the way it appeared like a ghost town, even though it wasn't. Where was everyone? Were they directed to stay inside if there was an outsider on campus?

Why did she feel the cold stare of unseen eyes? Barnabas's back was toward her, and she saw no one else. Still, she couldn't shake the feeling.

This place was strange—it left her unsettled.

Kind of like when she'd walked into DH-7 headquarters.

You should have let Ty or Mac know you were coming here. Always have backup.

But now Cassidy was in, and she needed to see what this place was about once and for all.

CHAPTER EIGHT

Barnabas led Cassidy into what looked like an old community center at the campground. Now it was just "The Meeting Place," as the crude, handmade wooden sign over the door read.

Her spine stiffened as she stepped inside and reality washed over her.

The man who ran this place was smart. He hadn't built any new buildings or done anything that would require a permit or inspection. Everything seemed to only have been fixed up cosmetically. The campers and trailers here were only temporary, so there were no county regulations for them.

Whoever ran this place appeared to know what he— or she—was doing.

The anxiety in Cassidy's stomach grew as she disappeared further from civilization—from her vehicle, from the gate where she could escape this place, from anyone who knew her.

You shouldn't have come here alone. The warning echoed in her mind again.

Wise is the person who realizes that strength can be found in numbers. Even wiser is the one who is choosy about who is a part of those numbers.

The Day-at-a-Glance quote echoed in her mind.

Cassidy took a moment to absorb the place. It reminded her of a summer camp she'd visited once, not as a camper but as part of a service project. No, the camps her parents had sent her to had been more like resorts.

Here, everything was rustic and any accessories appeared donated—the chairs with mauve cushions. A handmade podium on a handmade-looking stage. The walls were dark veneer paneling. A rectangular opening had been cut in the center of one wall and framed in to serve as a food passthrough. No doubt, that's where food was served. Cassidy could hear the rustle of someone cleaning dishes just out of sight.

The place smelled like grilled cheese and cafeteria food. It felt quiet and solemn. The dim light didn't add ambiance as much as it made the room feel dated and neglected. However, everything looked clean and maintained.

In the distance, Cassidy spotted a woman pushing out a mop and yellow bucket on wheels from the bathroom. She quickly glanced up at Cassidy before jerking her gaze back down and continuing to clean the floor.

Cassidy paused for long enough to soak her in. The woman was petite with light-brown hair. Curly. Down to her waist. She looked youngish—probably in her early twenties. She wore a beige tunic and khaki bottoms, just like the other people Cassidy had seen around here.

Why had the woman averted her gaze? Was she simply insecure? Or was there more to this? She almost seemed … submissive.

"Up this way," Barnabas's voice pulled her thoughts from the woman.

Cassidy looked over and saw him standing at the base of a dark stairway, motioning to her and appearing annoyed.

Cassidy followed him up a set of stairs behind the stage area. The steps groaned under her weight, and a dank smell filled her nostrils.

She gripped the railing as more memories of going undercover with DH-7 filled her mind. DH-7 was one of the deadliest gangs in the US. Cassidy had accidentally killed their leader, and there had been a manhunt out for her.

Finally, that nightmare was over. The gang had disbanded. The leaders were behind bars. Most of them, at least.

But the memories of her time undercover wouldn't stop coming. The fear. The intensity. The risk.

Cassidy hadn't been sure she would get out of the situation alive. She'd been buried so deeply in the underbelly of danger, she could have easily died.

This place looked different. The people looked different. But the risk felt the same.

At the top of the stairs, a short, narrow hallway came into view. Just like the stairway, it was dark and felt haunted by times past.

The bad feeling in Cassidy's gut continued to grow.

Finally, Barnabas stopped by a door—one of three in the hallway—and knocked. He muttered a few words to someone inside before ushering her into the room.

A man stood up from an oversized desk there.

Cassidy quickly took him in. He was probably in his mid-thirties with short, dark hair. A bright, confident smile lit his face. He wore slacks with an electric-blue button-up shirt—a very different look from the rest of the crowd here.

"I'm Anthony Gilead." He extended his hand.

Hesitantly, she shook it. "Police Chief Cassidy Chambers."

"I've heard wonderful things about you, Cassidy— can I call you that? Or do you prefer Chief Chambers?" His voice was as smooth as Lisa's honey-and-cinnamon-butter spread.

"Chief Chambers is great." She made certain to keep her voice professional. This wasn't a social call, and she didn't want the man to be too comfortable.

He nodded for her to sit down in the chair across from him. "Very well, then."

Lowering herself onto the fake-leather seat, she stared at Gilead as he smiled at her. Something about him made her feel like she was being sold an overpriced car by a very skilled salesman. She needed to give the man the benefit of the doubt, though.

"I didn't realize you'd heard anything about me," she stated. "I haven't seen you out and about in town."

The plastic smile still stretched across his face. "I prefer to keep things simple and limit my circle. There's a lot to be said for simplicity, you know."

How did they get supplies? Food? Equipment?

"I agree." She quickly scanned his office. Motivational sayings lined the walls—each quote attributed to himself. There were no personal pictures or awards. However, Cassidy did spot a cell phone peeking out from underneath a book.

Interesting. How did electronics tie in with the peaceful life they had here? Did Gilead allow others on the premises to carry the devices? Or did he have different standards for himself—as his clothes seemed to indicate.

"I've heard you brought a lot of peace and order to the town." He laced his fingers together in front of him as he addressed Cassidy. "Before you, the police chief was a bit of a joke."

Cassidy quickly inhaled, a touch of apprehension pounding in her veins. He knew about Chief Bozeman ... who'd left near the end of last summer.

"It definitely sounds like you've been talking to people." Which was strange since she'd never seen the man in town.

He flashed another pearly white smile, the action looking as easy as the sunrise. "No, I just do my homework."

"And why would you do homework about Lantern Beach?"

"I had to know if it was a safe place to come and bring people who are important to me."

"I see." It was the perfect response—executed with the ease of a well-practiced prison doctor with expert skills in lethal injection.

She glanced beyond Gilead and through the window there. The man had a view of the entire campground from his perch up here. Had he planned it that way? So he could keep an eye on everything—and everyone?

Cassidy cleared her throat. "Can you tell me about this place?"

"Not much to tell." He glanced around and flicked his hand, as if his kingdom was no big deal when, in fact, he definitely perceived himself as royalty. "It's a retreat center—much like the one your husband started."

She drew in another quick breath. "You know about that also?"

"Yes. As I said, I do my homework. Your husband helps those with broken spirits and bodies. We're not all that different now, are we? We both are just trying to make the world a better place."

A chill washed over her. This man had looked into her background entirely more than she was comfortable with.

Cassidy didn't respond to his question. "So this is a retreat center? Who comes here?"

"People who are down on their luck. Who are wrestling with life. Who need a fresh start. We offer that. We help them to get back on their feet."

"And they can leave any time they want?" She watched his expression carefully.

That grin appeared again, but it didn't quite reach Gilead's eyes.

"Of course they can. We're not monsters. We're not a military institute. We're a place of healing." He paused and studied her without apology. "You'd be a great asset to our community, you know."

Cassidy ignored his statement and, instead, pulled out her phone and showed him a picture. "Have you ever seen this man?"

"May I?" Gilead reached for her phone, a questioning look in his eyes as he waited for her approval.

Reluctantly, Cassidy let him hold it. There was something about this man she just didn't trust. It was almost as if she feared he'd touch the phone and somehow absorb all the information inside. The fear was incredibly off-balance. But the feeling wouldn't leave her.

He grunted and handed the phone back. "No, I can't say I've ever seen him."

"So you're saying he wasn't staying here," she clarified.

"No, I didn't say that. I don't have contact with everyone who comes here for help. I'm just saying the man doesn't look familiar to me." Each word sounded controlled, slow, and purposeful.

"And no one who's been staying here has gone missing?" Her words were equally as purposeful.

"No, of course not." Gilead leaned back and rested an ankle on his knee, as if doing a TV interview and trying to appear casual and relaxed—*trying* being the key word. "You think this man is a part of my group here?"

"You mean, your retreat center?"

"Yes, that's what I meant. Why does it matter? It's semantics, really."

"Because 'group' implies something different than retreat center." She refused to let this man have the upper hand.

His eyes darkened but only for a moment.

"I'm saying that no one here has gone missing." Gilead stood and tugged at the sleeves of his shirt. "Now, if you don't mind, I have things I need to do, Cassidy—I mean, Chief Chambers. I'll have my assistant show you out."

Cassidy wasn't done here, but she knew she wouldn't be getting any more answers from this man. Not now, at least.

As she took a step away, Gilead called to her one last time. Cassidy pivoted, her nerves still on edge.

With calm, cool motions, Gilead extended one hand, almost as if imitating a painting of Jesus that Cassidy had once seen, one in which He reached out to welcome lost sinners into His fold.

"Remember, there's always a place for you here,

Cassidy," Gilead said. "I could help you in your healing."

"My healing?" What in the world was he talking about?

"I see the torrent of pain and fear in the depths of your eyes. You've been through something traumatic, something that totally changed your life. And I can tell you're having a hard time getting over it. I have programs that could guide you and make you a new person."

A shiver crept up her spine at his words.

This man would not get to her.

Yet, at the same time, he already felt dangerously close to doing just that.

———

AFTER LEAVING her encounter with Gilead, Cassidy knew she needed to decompress—if only for a moment. And there was no one she'd rather do that with than Ty. He just happened to be at a good stopping place with his work on the cabanas—at least, that was what he'd said.

As he prepared some coffee for them, Cassidy put in a quick call with the North Carolina State Bureau of Investigation. She needed to know if statewide law enforcement had their eye on this Anthony Gilead guy and, if so, what they knew. An agent there promised to call her back.

Ty emerged from the house with two cups in his

hands. She drew in a quick breath at the sight of him. He wore his jeans—old ones that he worked in, but they still looked good on him. On his feet were his signature cowboy boots that reminded her he was a Texas boy at heart. His black, long-sleeved T-shirt was tight enough to show his sculpted abs and arms.

And he was hers. All hers.

She valued her husband's advice, even if she only had forty-five minutes until she had to be back at the office. At least the sun was cooperating as it shone down on them, offsetting the chilly midday breeze.

She finished telling Ty about her experience today with Gilead. Her gut told her this could be bigger than one island could handle, though it was too soon to say for sure.

"What are you thinking?" Ty sat beside her on the deck swing, which gently swayed back and forth, while Kujo sat at their feet. "What's your gut tell you about this guy?"

Another chill ran through Cassidy as she remembered Gilead's words to her before she left. *I see the torrent of pain and fear in the depths of your eyes. You've been through something traumatic, something that totally changed your life. And I can tell you're having a hard time getting over it.*

Mind games, she told herself. He was just playing mind games with her.

Cassidy shifted to face her husband. "Ty, I know a little about the mind-set behind people in gangs and cults and the like. Raul—the leader of DH-7—could be very charismatic and convincing. He had a personality that people wanted to follow. And they did follow him —to the point where they were willing to give up their lives."

Ty's gaze flickered with both wisdom and experience. "And you think this Gilead guy has those same qualities?"

"I do. Let's face it, religion is a great breeding ground for people who are in search of power."

He leaned forward, his elbows on his knees, and listened. "What do you mean?"

Cassidy tried to choose her words wisely, but she never felt like she had to be on guard with what she said around Ty. Still, the subject was delicate. "Look at how many people practically worship their pastors. They never question them or doubt them. The pastors are up so high on a pedestal that they can do whatever they want. Not every church or every pastor is like that. I know that. But there are plenty who are. Some people are just desperate for someone to follow."

"And that's not always the pastor's fault."

"Absolutely. I'm not pointing my finger at every pastor out there. I'm just saying that there are people in this world who are willing to take advantage of people who are hurting and who are looking for someone to lead them." She hadn't grown up in church, and she hadn't had a lot of negative experiences. In fact, her experience at church here on Lantern Beach had been wonderful and life-changing. But she'd been around the block enough to know that not everyone could say that.

She'd seen abuse within the church walls in her job as a detective.

"I agree. Not everyone in church leadership has the best of intentions. I've seen some ugly stuff myself. In fact, my church back in Texas had to fire their finance guy because he was embezzling money. There's sin, and it's everywhere—in church and outside of it."

She took another sip of her coffee. "I guess I'm just saying that this is how cults get started. People blindly following other people. And the members? They're usually people who are at the end of their rope—the most vulnerable in society. They're desperate, with nowhere else to go and no other hope."

Her words led to a moment of silence as the seriousness of the situation washed over them.

"So what now?" Ty finally asked.

Cassidy shook her head, feeling burdened. Her whole encounter today had gotten to her and only deepened the trepidation building inside her. "I don't know. I wish I did. But all of this is just getting started."

"Maybe you'll get more answers when Al's wife gets into town."

"Maybe. I can only hope." Cassidy's phone rang. When she saw the message, she frowned and stood.

"What is it?" Ty asked.

"With everything going on, I totally forgot someone was coming in today to interview for the position on the force."

"It's a good thing the station isn't far away."

"I better get there now. I'll see you tonight."

"I'll fix dinner. Maybe some fish with a nice salad."

"That sounds perfect." A moment of normal was just what she needed.

Before she walked away, Ty grabbed her hand and pulled her toward him for a quick kiss. "I look forward to it."

CHAPTER NINE

Cassidy tried to compose herself before walking into the station. This would be her first time interviewing someone for employment, and she had to admit she felt a rush of nerves.

See? She wasn't the type to take over a business like her father's Fortune 500 company. Melva acted scared of her. Leggott wasn't reliable for any seriously dangerous situations. And Cassidy hadn't hired anyone in six months because she was too picky.

A certain amount of self-doubt was healthy. That was what she told herself. But this was never what she set out to do. She'd just wanted to be a detective. Leading an entire department was new to her, but she was determined not to let the people here on this island down.

It was one of the reasons she was being so picky. She'd carefully examined all the applications that had come in, and almost none of the candidates had been suitable.

Except maybe today's interviewee. He showed promise. Dedication. He had experience.

When she stepped inside the station, a man sitting in one of the plastic chairs in the waiting room rose to his feet and extended his hand. "Chief Chambers?"

Cassidy quickly studied the man. Tall. Broad. Dark hair cut short and neat. An olive complexion and a friendly smile.

She returned his smile and stepped forward to shake his hand. "You must be Dane Bradshaw."

His handshake was firm and confident. "Nice to meet you, ma'am."

"Ma'am" made Cassidy feel so old, when in reality she'd just turned twenty-nine. Dane had to be close to her age.

"Thanks for coming." She motioned for him to follow. "Come on into my office. Melva, I'm going to need a few minutes with no interruptions—unless it's an emergency."

Melva nodded in response and continued to knit a baby blanket for a new mom on the island. The woman had gray hair and a plump figure. Even though she was probably in her late-fifties, she gave off an old-fashioned grandmotherly vibe. Maybe it was the knitting and quilting projects Melva was constantly working on during the downtime here at the station that made her seem older than she was.

Once inside her office, Cassidy closed the door and directed Dane to a seat.

"How was your drive?" she started, grabbing a pad of paper where she'd jotted down some questions.

"Uneventful."

"Those are the best kind." She smiled, already liking the man. He had a mild-mannered way about him that probably put people at ease, yet he seemed strong and competent—on first impression, at least. "I'm so glad you could make it out here. You realize just how small a town Lantern Beach is, right? It would be quite a change from Cincinnati."

"I'm ready for a change." He sat up straight and didn't hesitate with his answer.

"Why's that?" What made a person like Dane want to pack up everything and come here?

Cassidy knew her own personal answer, but she was curious to hear what Dane had to say. Perhaps he was running from something also. Or hiding.

She sat down behind her desk and focused her full attention on him.

"It's always been my dream to live in a beach town," he said, his hands resting on his legs and his shoulders straight but relaxed. "I love surfing, and I love the laid-back lifestyle. I thought it would be a nice change of pace."

"Not as exciting as the big city." She studied him, watching his expression. The last thing she wanted was to hire someone who couldn't handle small-town island life. Someone who would pack up after a few months and retreat from this kind of living. She didn't want to go through this process again any sooner than she had to.

"I think I've had my fill of city life." He paused, the first sign of apprehension on his face. "Honestly, I was jumped on the way home from work one night by some friends of a guy I put behind bars. I was in the hospital for a week. It made me look at life from a different perspective, I suppose."

That made sense. Trauma could spark life changes—the same thought Cassidy had pondered when talking to Trisha Hartman. "I see."

Dane shifted. "But I understand you still have some excitement in town. I heard people on the ferry talking on the way here about a body that washed up yesterday."

"People here do like to talk. It's one of the challenges—and blessings—of small-town life."

"I think I can handle that. Me and my dog, Ranger."

"Ranger?" she questioned.

"He's a four-year-old boxer mix—and he's a police dog. Best drug enforcement officer I've ever met, to tell you the truth. He can sniff out illegal substances like no one's business. We're kind of a package deal."

Cassidy nodded. So far Dane had given good answers. And she liked the idea of having a police dog here in the department, though she would need to check into the legalities of that.

"If you're offered the position here, when would you be available to start?" Cassidy asked.

"As soon as you need me." Dane shifted. "I resigned from my job in Cincinnati a month ago, and I've been trying to figure out where I wanted to go. I packed up everything in my truck and have confidence I'll figure things out. The chief said he'd give you a reference for me, though. He understood why I needed to leave and why I wanted a change of pace."

Cassidy leaned forward, getting ready for the harder questions. The "what-if" scenarios.

But, based on what she knew so far, she thought she might have found her new officer—or officers, if she included Ranger.

———

AFTER THE INTERVIEW was done and Dane had left, Lisa called and told Cassidy she was back in town. They arranged to meet at The Crazy Chefette at 5:30. It worked out perfectly.

Cassidy was still feeling good about Dane when she pulled up to The Crazy Chefette. She'd promised him she would be in touch before the end of the week, but maybe she'd finally have some more help around here. If her theory about Anthony Gilead was correct, she might need it.

Her friend's cheeks looked flushed when Cassidy stepped inside the back door of the restaurant to where the kitchen area was located as well as a stairway leading up to Lisa's apartment.

"How did it go? Dress shopping, that is," Cassidy

said, wondering what the new scent in the restaurant was. She smelled something savory. Roast beef, maybe? Either way, her stomach grumbled.

Lisa grinned as she stood by the wooden staircase with an apron around her waist. "I found the perfect dress. Do you want to see?"

All of Cassidy's other pressing concerns disappeared for a second. Her friend was getting married. She didn't want to miss out on these moments. "Of course. I'd love to."

"Come with me." Lisa grabbed her hand and pulled her up the stairs to her apartment. There, hanging in the doorway, was a beautiful white wedding gown. "What do you think?"

Cassidy stepped closer as Lisa unzipped the clear bag surrounding it. "Lisa, it's beautiful. You're going to be such a gorgeous bride."

It was. The gown was pure white, sleeveless, and simple, with layers coming down from the waist. Lisa would be stunning in it.

Lisa beamed some more. "Thanks, Cassidy. All of this seems surreal."

"I can imagine." Cassidy leaned against the doorframe, grateful for a moment of normalcy. "Speaking of which, how is Braden doing?"

Cassidy really wanted to hire him before the busy summer season started. She'd hire him now, if she could, but she knew Braden needed more time to heal.

"He's doing great. Now that his medications are straight, it's made a world of difference in him."

"I'm glad to hear that." The two seemed so happy together.

"Me too. Braden is amazing, and I'm so glad we found each other. It's like people say, it happens when you least expect it."

"You guys seem incredibly happy. I'm thrilled for you."

Lisa's smile slipped and she straightened. "As much as I'd love to think this is merely a social call, I know you didn't stop by just to see my dress."

"I didn't—even though I'm really glad I got to see it."

"But you need to see that ... that ... thing in my freezer. No disrespect to the body. But it's in my restaurant." Lisa offered an exaggerated frown. "Any idea how much longer? I'm still afraid word is going to leak about this and people will start thinking I'm going all *Fargo* here."

"You mean, that you're serving freshly roasted ... human. Is that what that smell is?"

Lisa's mouth dropped open. "It's pork tenderloin. You don't really—"

Cassidy raised her hand, holding back a smile. "I'm just joking. Sorry. I shouldn't have gone there."

Lisa's shoulders slumped with relief. "Not funny."

"Sorry." Cassidy shook her head. "Anyway, I know Doc Clemson is having someone come out this week to fix the one at the morgue. But you know how hard it can be to get people out here."

Lisa frowned. "Yes, I do. Come on. I'm keeping the

freezer locked, just like Doc requested."

Back downstairs, Cassidy stepped into the freezer. Her heart skipped a beat when she saw the body there. She was a cop. She should be used to seeing things like this. Yet she never did get used to it.

She pulled on some gloves before unzipping the white bag around the presumed Al Hartman. She bit back disgust at seeing the frozen, dead body with its purplish tint. Working quickly, she looked at the man's lower abdomen.

Sure enough, there was a small mark there.

A mark that was probably made when Al had his appendix out. She doubled-checked behind his ear also and found the birthmark that Trisha had told her about.

It looked like the deceased really was Al Hartman.

Tomorrow, Cassidy would talk to his estranged wife and find out more information. Maybe she could piece together how the man had ended up here on the island. How he'd wound up dead with those scars on his back.

Her phone buzzed just then.

"Chief, we've got a call," Melva said.

"What this time?"

"Eddie Anderson, Louise's boy, he apparently jumped the fence over at that new Gilead's Cove community," she said. "One of his friends dared him. Anyway, he was shot at but managed to get away unscathed. He's at the station now shaking like a wet dog outside in the winter."

Cassidy pressed her lips together before saying, "I'll be right there."

CHAPTER TEN

Cassidy quickly observed Eddie Anderson as he sat across from her in her office.

The sixteen-year-old was a bit of a troublemaker. He had a wild streak that came out whenever he got bored. And in the winter, he got bored a lot here on the island, where there were no movie theaters or other amusements to occupy people who needed to stay busy.

He was tall and lanky, with an acne-freckled face, dark hair styled in a buzz cut, and a defiant look in his eyes.

Right now, his mom sat beside him. She was the opposite of Eddie—short and plump, with brittle, graying hair that came down to her shoulders. Her eyes didn't show defiance but fear.

A pang of compassion rushed through Cassidy as she sensed the woman's worry and distress for her son.

"Why don't you start at the beginning, Eddie?"

Cassidy folded her hands together in front of her. "Tell me what happened tonight."

"Tell her what you told me." His mom nudged him with her elbow.

Some of the defiance left his eyes, showing the boy who was still buried deep inside him—the one he tried to hide by acting macho and by doing stupid stuff.

"My friend dared me to jump the fence at the old campground," he started, his gaze shifty. "I didn't think it was a big deal. Just a campground, right? Besides, I'd been curious about who was staying there since it seems so hush-hush."

"What happened after you jumped the fence?"

"I told my friend—Mark Zinck, since I'm sure you're wondering. He can verify my story—I told him I'd take some pictures to prove that I'd done it. I had my camera ready. And everything was good at first. I mean, it was quiet. I almost didn't think anyone was there. It was kind of weird since I knew there *were* people there."

"And then?" Cassidy knew this story would take a turn for the worse, and she tried to brace herself.

"So I was walking around. Mostly, there were old campers. Not much to look at. But as I got to the other side of the place—near the water—I saw a campfire." His eyes stilled, as if he was remembering something tragic.

"What was happening around this campfire?" Cassidy asked, her breath suspended with anticipation.

Eddie closed his eyes for a moment. "There were

three men. One had this stick in his hands, but it wasn't wooden. It was straight—maybe iron. He stuck it into the fire then pressed it into the other man's back. It reminded me of branding cattle or something. Isn't that what it's called?"

Cassidy repressed a shiver as she pictured it playing out. "Yes, I believe so. Did the man seem willing? Or was this done to him by force?"

"No one was holding him down. But I could see the pain on his face. I freaked out. When I turned to leave, my foot hit an old water heater that had been left on the ground, and it made a loud sound. The men knew I was there and started chasing me. I knew I couldn't slow down or they might brand me also."

The boy must have been terrified. "Did they shoot at you?"

"Right when I got to the fence, one of them told me he was going to fire if I didn't freeze. I didn't care. I had to keep moving. When I dropped to the other side of the fence, I felt a bullet whiz by me."

"You only felt it?" Cassidy clarified. "You didn't hear anything?"

Fear shattered his voice. "No, I didn't. I figured they must have one of those silencer things."

"I take it the bullet missed you."

"That's right. And I didn't stick around any longer. I jumped in my car and went home."

"When he got there, I noticed something was wrong, and Eddie finally told me what happened," his mom said, the edges of her mouth pulling down in a worried frown. "I insisted we come here and talk to you."

"You did the right thing. I need to know about stuff like this happening here on the island. But I have to say that you shouldn't be trespassing, Eddie."

He frowned. "I know. I had no idea …"

"And they could have been perfectly in their rights to defend their property if they thought you were a threat to them." Cassidy hated to say the words, but they were true.

"But—"

"I'm not saying what they did—or what they were doing—was right. I'm just letting you know the law."

Meekly, he nodded. "I get it. Am I in trouble?"

"No, but consider this a warning. Don't go to Gilead's Cove again." Whatever was happening there, these people didn't want any outsiders to know about it.

The bad feeling churned harder in Cassidy's gut.

She needed to go there. Again. Right now.

Before she made it back to her SUV, her phone rang.

"What are you doing?" Ty asked. "I thought you'd be home by now. I have dinner ready."

Guilt washed over her. She'd never wanted to be someone who was married to her job. Yet that's how she felt right now. "I'm sorry, Ty. Something came up, and I meant to call you. I just … I got distracted. I'm so sorry."

"Everything okay?"

"I can explain more later. But right now I've got to go back to Gilead's Cove."

"Let me go with you." His voice changed from concerned to tense.

"Why would you go with me?" Ty usually stayed out of her work.

"I don't like that place. I don't like the feeling I get when I go by it. And I don't think it's a good idea that you go alone. I'd say take Leggott with you, but he doesn't exactly inspire confidence."

After a second of thought, Cassidy nodded. "Okay. Can you meet me here at the station in five?"

"I'm leaving now."

———

CASSIDY GRIPPED the steering wheel as she approached Gilead's Cove. The bad feeling in her gut grew—the feeling that something bad was brewing on the island. She'd set up a life for herself here over the past several months, and now she felt like everything was on the brink of shattering.

She couldn't let that happen, yet she partly felt powerless to stop it.

She glanced over at Ty, still confused by his insistence on being with her. "Is there more going on here than what you're telling me? This isn't like you to want to come with me."

Ty's jaw visibly clenched. "There's been a strange

man in town. I've seen him watching us. Or watching you. I don't know which."

Her spine straightened. "What? Tell me more."

"I saw him yesterday for the first time, but I thought maybe it was a coincidence. But then I saw him again earlier today when I stopped by the house Austin and Skye are restoring. It was just for a moment—he drove past, but I caught a glimpse of his face. I can't say this guy is anyone dangerous, to be truthful. But I can't stop thinking about DH-7."

"Does he look like a gang member?"

"No, but, as you well know, not everyone who is affiliated with the gang looks like they are. This guy looks pretty average—middle-aged, casual dresser, Caucasian. I didn't see any tattoos. I feel like he's watching us."

"I think I saw that man yesterday at the crime scene," Cassidy said. "He was standing in the distance, on a dune, and he disappeared when I approached him."

"Sounds like the same guy."

She shivered. "You really think he's connected with the whole tragedy involving DH-7?"

Ty squeezed her knee. "I have no idea, Cassidy. I just know that I can't stand the thought of something happening to you."

She reached the entrance to Gilead's Cove and put her vehicle into park. Before getting down to business, she shifted in her seat. She reached over and touched

Ty's jaw and cheek, emotion swelling in her chest. "I'm sorry you're in the middle of my crazy life."

"I knew what I was signing up for when we got married," he said softly, his gaze fixated on hers. "And you better believe I'm going to be at your side in case you ever need me."

Warmth spread through her chest. "Thank you, Ty."

She leaned forward and planted a quick kiss on his lips.

But this was no time for romance. Right now they needed to figure out Gilead's Cove.

Gathering her energy, she rolled her window down, pressed the button at the guard station, and waited. A moment later, a voice came on the line. If she had to guess, it was Barnabas.

"Can I help you, Chief Chambers?"

So there was a camera here. Good to know. "I need to talk to someone about an incident that occurred here this evening."

"You're talking about the boy who trespassed on our property?"

Cassidy narrowed her eyes at his flippant words. "That's correct."

"We've decided not to press charges."

"That's … kind of you. But we still need to talk."

"I'm afraid it's after hours."

Irritation pinched at her back muscles. "And I'm afraid this is official police business."

Silence stretched until finally the voice said, "One minute."

Cassidy glanced at Ty and let out a sigh. "Security here is tighter than it is at the White House."

"Who exactly are they trying to keep out?" Ty asked.

"Or maybe the question should be: who are they trying to keep in?"

CHAPTER ELEVEN

Cassidy held her breath as the gate opened. A moment later, Barnabas appeared, carrying a lantern and looking rather primal under its glow.

She shivered.

He motioned for her to pull inside. As soon as she did, the gates closed. Hearing them click in place, she shivered again.

Thank goodness, Ty had insisted on coming with her. This place was bad enough during the daytime. At night, it was full-on creepy.

She rolled down her window and waited for Barnabas's next instruction.

"You'll need to leave your vehicle here again and follow me on foot," he said.

She'd barely had time to climb out before Barnabas started down the path toward the Meeting Place.

Cassidy and Ty quickly caught up and fell in step behind Barnabas. As they walked, she looked around.

Just as earlier, everything was quiet. Eerily quiet. Where were all of the people who stayed here? Why were none of them curious and peering out their doors to see who'd come to the compound for a visit?

She had no idea, but the conclusions that came together in her mind weren't good.

She counted the RVs. Just within her sight, there were thirty of them. If two people stayed in each, that would mean there could be sixty people here. Cassidy suspected there were more.

"Is this place giving you the creeps?" Ty whispered, his breath tickling her ear.

"Absolutely." Part of her felt like she was playing a deadly game and could be ambushed at any minute.

Their feet shuffled across the gravel path as darkness surrounded them. The only light came from the lantern and from the crescent moon above. Finally, they stopped at the Meeting Place. Barnabas unlocked the door and ushered them into the dark building.

Another shiver captured Cassidy.

She was the police chief. She wasn't supposed to feel spooked.

Yet she was definitely feeling that way.

"Gilead will be down in a moment," Barnabas announced.

He walked away, up the stairs, and all the light disappeared from the room.

Just as Cassidy turned to say something else to Ty, she felt movement beside her.

She reached for her gun.

"I didn't mean to frighten you," a deep voice said.

Another lantern roared to life, and Gilead's face came into view beside them. A strange smile played across his lips as he stared at Cassidy and Ty.

Cassidy left her gun in the holster and resisted the impulse to reach for Ty, who stood beside her. If she showed any weakness, she felt certain Gilead would pounce on it and exploit it.

"I wasn't expecting anyone at this hour, so excuse me for the welcome." Gilead pointed to some wooden chairs huddled in the corner in the distance. "Let's have a seat, shall we?"

"I prefer to stand," Cassidy said. Standing would make it clear this wasn't an invitation for Gilead to try and convert her again.

"Very well, then." Gilead's gaze shifted to Ty. "And who is this here with you?"

Ty's muscles visibly bristled as he stood like a soldier poised for action. Having him here with her made Cassidy feel a hundred times safer. Cassidy had no doubt that he'd give his life to protect her.

Cassidy cleared her throat. "This is Ty Chambers, and he's—"

"Your husband," Gilead interrupted, satisfaction stretching across his gaze. "That's so special that you two can work together, whether it's official or unofficial."

Another shiver raked across her spine. Gilead had researched Cassidy and Ty, just like he'd researched Lantern Beach. She felt sure of it.

"As you probably are aware, the police department here on the island is short-staffed right now, so Ty is giving us a hand." It was no secret that they were undermanned. Certainly, Gilead had done enough research to know that, so Cassidy wasn't revealing too much.

"Like I said, that's very special. I love seeing strong couples who can work together. The bond between the two of you is so solid that I can nearly reach out and touch it."

Cassidy shoved aside his words. The man was good at reading people. If only that were a crime ... "I need to talk to you about an incident that occurred here this evening."

"I wondered if that might bring you out. What do you need? I believe Barnabas has already told you that we're not going to press charges this time. And in case you were thinking of pressing charges, need I remind you that we were just defending our property." He lowered the lantern, and the light scattered around the dark, cold room just a little more.

Gilead had explained it as easily as explaining how to set out a mouse trap. The man's unwavering self-control verged on being psychotic.

"He was just a teenage boy with bad judgment," Cassidy said. "You could have seriously hurt or killed him."

"We weren't aiming to harm him, just to scare him off."

"There are better ways to do that, ways that don't involve guns."

"We were perfectly within our rights. There are clearly signs outside the Cove telling people that this is private property and they should keep out."

Cassidy swallowed hard. The man was obviously well-researched. He knew the law—and that made him even more dangerous. She decided to veer into the next subject instead. "I wanted to speak with you about something this boy said he saw here. Apparently, there was a man being branded like livestock."

Gilead's eyes narrowed with doubt. "That's a harsh way to put it. We prefer to call it being marked. It's not unlike getting a tattoo or a piercing. It just sounds harsher."

Because it was inhumane. Cassidy wasn't going to excuse it that easily. "I'd like to speak to the man who was 'marked.'"

"I'm not sure that's possible." An unreadable emotion flickered in his gaze.

"Why not?"

"He's resting."

"Then you can wake him up. Otherwise, I'm going to need to bring you into the station and launch an investigation. Physically harming and assaulting someone is a crime. We have a witness to verify it happened."

"But no charges have been filled because everyone involved was a willing participant. Certainly you don't go around arresting tattoo artists and those who pierce ears?"

"Another person was mutilated."

A frown quickly flickered across his lips. "Like I said, it's nothing more than a tattoo."

"I'd still like to speak to this man and verify that." Cassidy held his gaze, unwilling to back down.

Gilead didn't say anything for a moment until he finally nodded. "Very well, then. Barnabas, I need you to go get Kaleb for me."

"Yes, sir."

Like a ghost, Barnabas appeared from somewhere in the back of the building and scurried outside.

Had the man been nearby, simply listening and waiting to be at Gilead's beck and call? Was this leader so charismatic that he could talk people into doing whatever he wanted? Cassidy suspected the answer was yes.

Gilead turned back toward them after a few seconds of silence stretched. "So how long have the two of you been married?"

No way would Cassidy willingly share anything with this man. He'd use any information against her. She felt sure of it.

"I prefer not to talk about my personal life," Cassidy said.

"I understand. I too like my privacy. And I also promise that privacy to all of my guests here."

The man irritated Cassidy. He had an answer for everything—and those answers came a little too easily.

Like he'd planned them. Formulated them in advance. He thought he was smarter than everyone else in the room, and those kinds of people really got under her skin.

She wanted to steal a look at Ty and get his read on the situation. But this wasn't the time. Gilead was too observant, and she didn't want the man to know anything more about her than he already did.

"You hold yourself like someone with a military background," Gilead said, turning to Ty.

Cassidy stiffened. The man had known about Hope House. He'd looked into Ty's background also, hadn't he?

Ty's jaw was rigid and his demeanor steely and protective as he said, "Is that right?"

"I'm guessing special forces," Gilead continued. "Your eyes have the intelligence for it, and you're obviously physically fit enough for the tasks required."

Ty said nothing.

"I can only imagine the things you've seen," Gilead said.

"I'm not here to talk about myself," Ty said.

"Very well, then."

Cassidy shivered as another wave of cold washed over her. The room was so chilly, and the darkness only added to it. The place … it almost felt like a grave—a place devoid of warmth, of hope, of life.

She prayed for wisdom in handling this situation before it got out of control.

CHAPTER TWELVE

After what seemed like hours, Barnabas returned,
another man beside him.

Kaleb appeared to be in his thirties, with a square
face and eyes that wouldn't settle—the man's gaze shot
back and forth, like he didn't know where to look.

Barnabas didn't hold onto the man's arm, but
Cassidy felt as if he did. She couldn't describe the feeling, only that Barnabas seemed to have some kind of
control over Kaleb without actually touching him.

"Chief Chambers, this is Kaleb," Gilead said.
"Kaleb, Chief Chambers has some questions for you."

Kaleb stepped closer, his gaze downcast. "What can
I do for you?"

"Can you state your first and last name for me?"

"Kaleb Walker."

"How old are you, Kaleb?"

"Twenty-seven."

"And where are you from?"

"I live here." Kaleb glanced at Gilead, who seemed to give his silent approval.

"Can you tell me about the incident that happened here tonight?" Cassidy continued.

"Yes, ma'am. I chose to be marked, to show I'm a part of this community. It's a great honor to carry the mark of Gilead."

She repressed a shiver. "A great honor. Why?"

"Because it means I'm officially a part of the group here. I've passed the initial initiation with members of the Council."

Cassidy glanced at Gilead and raised an eyebrow. "Initial initiation?"

Gilead shrugged. "It's nothing, really. Just something to prove that members have the means and know-how to stay here and help provide for the community. We believe everyone should carry their own weight. If not, we ask that they return to where they came from."

"I see." She turned back to Kaleb. "May I see your mark?"

Kaleb looked back at Gilead again, who nodded. Once he was approved, Kaleb tugged his tunic up. He winced as the shirt brushed across his back.

Branded on his left shoulder was a symbol of some sort.

Cassidy squirmed at the sight of it. The mark itself looked deep. The edges of his skin were swollen and crisp. Blisters had begun to form around the burn.

The whole ordeal had to be incredibly painful.

Cassidy could only imagine what it had felt like to have the scorching hot metal press against his skin.

Quickly, she scanned the rest of his back for any scars or other signs that he'd been whipped like their victim who'd washed ashore.

She saw nothing.

"Are you satisfied now, Chief?" Gilead asked.

"I suppose."

"Very well, then. If you don't mind, Barnabas will be escorting you back to your vehicle. It's our time of rest. After a hard day's labor, everyone is tired. It's the good kind of tired. Proverbs 13:4 says that a sluggard's appetite is never filled, but the desires of the diligent are fully satisfied. Sleep is the satisfying reward of the diligent, wouldn't you say?"

"I agree."

But Cassidy didn't like the feeling in her gut as she walked away.

———

TY CLENCHED his hands into fists as he climbed back into Cassidy's SUV. He waited until they were out of the gate to say anything.

"That place rubs me wrong in all kinds of ways," he said.

"Me too." Cassidy stared straight ahead, her hands white-knuckled on the steering wheel. "What did you think of that mark on Kaleb's back?"

"It almost reminded me of a Hebrew letter or something."

"I wondered that also. I'm going to try and look it up. Maybe talk to Pastor Jack."

"Good idea." Ty shook his head, trying to best articulate what he was feeling. "I can't put my finger on it, Cassidy, but there's something about that Gilead guy …"

"He knows more about us than he should."

"And that scares me. But there's more. I almost … I don't know. I know it might sound strange, but I almost feel like I've met him before."

She stole a glance at Ty, a knot between her eyes. "It was dark. Maybe he just had that kind of voice."

"Maybe. But I'm not convinced that's true." Ty's jaw tightened as he remembered their conversation. "That question he asked me about being in the military? It was pointed, Cassidy. It wasn't an observation, but he was trying to watch for my reaction."

Her lips pressed together. "I had that impression also."

"And then there are those scars on your victim's back. That reminds me of someone I rescued over in Iraq. A soldier who'd been taken captive and tortured."

At his words, Cassidy pulled off to the side of the road and turned toward him. Strands of her hair escaped from her bun and were illuminated by the overhead glow of light. "You think my victim has a connection to you?"

"No, I'm not trying to say that, necessarily. I just think … that we need to proceed very cautiously."

"We?" Cassidy questioned.

He stared out the window, all his Navy SEAL training rushing back to him.

At Gilead's Cove, Ty had felt like he was on one of his missions and charged with protecting the people under his care. He'd tried to put his warrior side behind him, but it rustled to life now as pure instinct took over.

"Of course I want you to do your job, Cassidy," Ty finally said. "I don't want to interfere. But there's no way I want you anywhere close to that guy without me being with you. Promise me."

She stole another glance at him, her eyes narrow with concern, before nodding. "Okay, I promise. I can tell you feel strongly about this."

"Something is going on here on this island, Cassidy. And I don't like it one bit."

CHAPTER THIRTEEN

Hunger gripped Moriah's stomach.

She wasn't used to not being able to eat when she wanted. But here, everyone only ate at breakfast, lunch, and dinner. The schedule taught them self-control.

And there was no food to get anywhere else. There were no snack machines or stores. Each resident here got only one serving from the kitchen during mealtimes. That was it.

After everyone finished eating together, the kitchen crew came and took the plates. There was no chance to save any leftovers and take them back to her trailer.

But Moriah was hungry.

It was early morning, but if she went into the kitchen, maybe she could sneak a piece of bread—just something small to ease the grumbles in her stomach.

However, it was more than that. She felt shaky. Hypoglycemia had been a part of her life for the past three years. Sometimes, she just needed to eat in order to keep her blood sugar in check. Certainly Gilead would understand.

After getting dressed, she stepped out of her RV.

It was still dark outside, and a bitterly cold wind greeted her. She needed a coat. She wanted one. She'd always hated to be cold. Her mom had said she was born with ice in her veins.

But she would be strong and suffer to show her dedication to the cause. She would utilize mind over matter—just like Gilead had talked about yesterday during an afternoon enlightenment session. There were two per day, not including the morning prayer.

Yesterday's session had reminded Moriah about why she was here. Gilead could speak into her life like no one else ever had been able to. It was as if he could see her soul and knew what she needed to hear.

As she hastened her steps, her conviction grew. She could practice the power of making right choices—whether that was with eating, feeling cold, or overcoming past struggles.

That was right—overcoming. She was an overcomer.

She was going to move beyond her past. Move beyond the labels people had given her. *White trash. Loser. Not worth a person's time.*

Those were the nice insults. She'd heard far worse.

Everyone here had been so welcoming. No one looked at her with pity.

Somewhere in the distance, a stick broke.

She froze.

Was someone out there? Watching her?

Her lungs tightened, and she slunk from the center of the road to the edge. There were more shadows here to conceal her.

But she had to be careful.

When she heard nothing else, she continued.

There had been a commotion here last night, and Moriah wondered what that was about. She'd heard voices. Had seen lights. Certainly Gilead would explain what had happened during one of today's sessions. There wasn't anything to be worried about.

Her hands trembled. She really needed something to eat.

Finally, she reached the Meeting Place. She tugged at the door and it opened.

Thankfully.

She quietly stepped into the building and started toward the kitchen.

Halfway there, she heard voices and froze.

What if someone caught her?

They'll understand. You have a medical condition.

Hunger propelled her actions. She was going to be an overcomer, but she couldn't afford not to grab a little food. It was a necessity, not a desire.

She slipped into the kitchen and hid behind the wall next to the doorway, praying she wasn't caught.

They'd understand.

Yet she didn't feel confident of that. And she couldn't afford to get kicked out. No, she needed to be here.

"Don't worry—we have someone in place to handle this."

That voice was Gilead's, Moriah realized. Who was he speaking with? Where were they?

"Will one person masquerading in town—blending in—be enough to keep us one step ahead of the police?" someone else said.

"Yes, we'll know exactly what's going on in the town," Gilead said. "There will be no surprises."

"Good—because the police chief looked nosy."

"Nothing is going to get in our way. God has ordained for us to be here, and He will provide for us. This is simply a precaution—like God sending Joshua and Caleb into Canaan to see if the ground was fertile, as we read in the book of Numbers."

"Yes, Teacher. That makes sense. This person—our Caleb, our spy—will report back to us and let us know if anyone in town is suspicious."

"Exactly. It should work out well for all of us."

The voices faded—going upstairs, it sounded like.

Gilead really wanted to protect this area, Moriah realized. It was important to him that everyone retain their privacy, a fact she deeply appreciated.

If the government got involved, things would go south. Officials would try to dictate how they operated and who could be here. She'd seen it in action before. They couldn't let that happen.

Her respect and admiration for Gilead grew.

He was their protector—and she desperately wanted a protector in her life.

Quickly, she grabbed some bread from a tray in the back of the kitchen. She shoved it in her mouth, eating as quickly as possible.

After wiping the telltale crumbs from her shirt, she paused. She would just take the rest of this loaf back with her. That way, if she ever needed food again, she wouldn't have to sneak here to get it. No, she'd keep it somewhere safe in her room.

But she had to be careful. Because there were many rules here at Gilead's Cove.

And with those rules also came punishment.

CHAPTER FOURTEEN

Cassidy hadn't been able to sleep all night. Her mind was full of too many questions, especially after she'd gotten the picture that Trisha Hartman sent her of Al last evening.

He looked like an exact match to their John Doe.

Cassidy had also talked to Pastor Jack. She'd sketched a picture of the mark on Kaleb's back and showed it to him. He thought the symbol looked like the Hebrew symbol "M." His answer had been more complicated than that since the Hebrew and English alphabet didn't match exactly. But at least it was something to start with.

She was creeping closer to answers, but Cassidy still had a lot of work to do.

Before the sun even rose, she went into the office and put in a request to assess Al Hartman's finances. It would take a little while for the request to go through. But those results could tell her a lot about the man.

At eight, the agent from the North Carolina State Bureau of Investigation would arrive.

Later on, Al Hartman's estranged wife would come.

Cassidy also needed to get back with Dane and tell him he'd gotten the job. She knew he was staying on the island overnight, and she wanted to catch him before he left.

Sometime in between all that, she wanted to talk to the realtor who'd sold that land to Anthony Gilead. She wasn't sure she'd get any rest at all on the island with that man here. No, this island was supposed to be a sanctuary. It was a safe place where people came to find themselves or to find peace—whichever came first.

What it wasn't was a place where an evil man could hide out and hurt other people—with or without their permission.

She had no proof Gilead was evil. He'd covered his tracks nicely. But the moment he slipped up and Cassidy could prove it, he would be in her custody.

Just as she took a sip of her coffee, she heard a pounding on the door. As she poked her head out, she spotted Serena waving at her from the other side of the glass-front entry.

Serena was the college-aged niece of Cassidy's friend Skye. The girl changed personalities like most people changed clothes. Serena had taken over Elsa, the ice cream truck that Cassidy had operated when she'd first moved here.

Today, Serena was dressed like cotton candy—in pink from head to toe. Her hair was even in pigtails, which made her look much younger than her twenty-one years. No doubt the girl had seen Cassidy's car out front and had decided to stop by for a quick morning chat. It wasn't entirely unusual.

"Hey, Serena. What's going on?" Cassidy let the girl inside.

"I met someone." Serena's face glowed and matched her outfit.

"Did you? That's exciting. Who is this guy?"

"His name is Dietrich, and he just moved to the island."

Cassidy smiled, finding Serena's enthusiasm to be contagious. "How did you meet?"

"He's staying at a house on the island, and I was selling ice cream. He came out to buy some. He asked me if I would come every day, so I did. We started talking and *boom!* I think we really hit it off."

"Has he asked you out?"

Serena made a face. "Well, no. Not really. But he's going to. I can feel it."

"Well, I hope he does. He must be a fisherman if he came here to vacation in March."

She shrugged. "I'm not really sure. I didn't ask. I mean, he doesn't look like a fisherman. He looks like Ryan Reynolds, if you ask me."

What had the two of them talked about? Ice cream? Serena didn't seem to know that much about the man.

"Do you know how I know he's the one?" Serena continued, her eyes sparkling with joy.

"Please tell." Cassidy couldn't wait to hear Serena's take on love.

"Elsa keeps spontaneously playing 'How Sweet It Is to Be Loved by You' whenever Dietrich is around."

Many people on the island still thought that Elsa the ice cream truck had a mind of her own. It was ridiculous. What Elsa had was a short in her wires. Ty had fixed it when Serena bought the vehicle, but Serena had asked him to "un-fix it." She thought the rumors that the ice cream truck was haunted added to the charm of buying from her. She'd even set up an Instagram account for the truck.

Just as Serena took a step to the door, Cassidy spotted the NCSBI agent pull up.

"I'd love to talk more, but I do have an appointment," Cassidy said. "Keep me updated on what happens, okay?"

"Will do!" And with a flutter of her hand, Serena was off, skipping away like she didn't have a care in the world.

And, for a moment, Cassidy envied her.

———

FIVE MINUTES LATER, Cassidy and Agent Gabe Abbott were seated across from each other with coffee in hand. Melva had come in to monitor the front desk, so Cassidy's door was now closed.

"Thanks so much for coming, Agent Abbott." It

made Cassidy feel better to know that the NCSBI, the State Police, Coast Guard, and marine police were all nearby to back her up when needed.

"Please, call me Gabe." Gabe appeared to be in his late forties with short blond hair and a squarish face. She'd met a couple NCSBI agents before, but never Gabe.

"I trust you had a good trip here."

"I actually came in late last night. It's a good thing I did. I heard the ferry was shut down this morning because of rough waters."

"That happens around here. Safety first." Cassidy hadn't heard about the ferry, but she made a mental note that Trisha Hartman might not be able to get here on schedule. That was too bad—even though Cassidy had already concluded that their John Doe was most likely her estranged husband.

Gabe shifted. "Your phone call has me curious."

"We have a curious situation on our island." Cassidy didn't waste any time. She explained to Gabe how the old campground had been purchased, about Anthony Gilead, and all the strange goings-on that had occurred there. Gabe listened, not saying anything until she finished.

"It's a very interesting situation, and I'm glad you brought it to our attention. When you sent me the name 'Gilead's Cove' as well as 'Anthony Gilead,' I started doing some research. Coincidentally, there's no Anthony Gilead that I can find record of."

"Really? So he's using an alias …"

"It would appear that way. And, as you know, that's not a crime in itself, unless he legally misrepresents himself under another identity or assumes someone else's identity."

"Correct."

"It's a possibility that he's recently changed his name, so I've put in requests for court records in other states. That process could be lengthy."

"I appreciate your effort."

Gabe shifted. "However, I have been researching Gilead's Cove, and I found out some interesting things that I thought you might like to know. I inquired with some other law enforcement agencies, including the FBI and local law enforcement in some neighboring states."

"I'm all ears." Cassidy straightened, anxious to hear what he had to say.

"A movement started in West Virginia about two years ago," he said. "It was a church group—or so authorities thought. It didn't seem like a big deal, but the numbers started to grow. It was led by someone named … Anthony Gilead."

"Ah ha. So there was a record of him." And this was another connection to West Virginia—the same state Trisha Hartman was from.

"Exactly. This man is fascinating. He's apparently a charismatic guy who could sell a glass of water to a drowning man. People wanted to follow him and believe in his message. In fact, they'd do more than that.

He convinced them to give up everything to be a part of a retreat center he was running."

"Sounds eerie." Cassidy took another sip of her coffee.

"Doesn't it, though? The crazy part is that people were doing it. They were embracing this new way of life that he presented to them—one that was simple and where everyone was equal."

"I have to admit, I could see where those ideas have their appeal." She'd been in the rat race before, and she preferred a slower way of life herself.

"I can see it also. Authorities only learned about Gilead's Cove when family members of some of the new 'recruits' started coming forward, concerned about their loved ones."

Cassidy leaned forward. "How many people are we talking? How big did this grow?"

"When it was in West Virginia, we were talking about one hundred people who were a part of the core group—the group that lived together. However, they also have others who don't live with the group. They're called scouts."

"Interesting."

"The core group outgrew the land there. In the blink of an eye, they up and disappeared, and no one was sure where they went. Until I got your phone call."

Cassidy tapped her finger against her desk in thought. "They came here. I wonder why Lantern Beach of all places."

"That's a great question."

She leaned back, still processing everything. "Do they appear to be dangerous?"

"Not that we can tell. There have never been any reports on anything illegal. They seem to be a peaceful group."

"No defectors that you've been able to talk to?" She needed the inside scoop.

"Again, not that we know of."

She sighed, thankful for the answers she'd gotten yet wishing for more. "Thank you for coming. I appreciate it. But this is a whole new experience for me. I'm still treading water here and trying to find out how to handle this."

"We're going to look into things and see if we can figure out this Anthony Gilead guy's real name. That would be a good starting place."

"I agree."

He stood. "And we'd appreciate you keeping us in the loop as much as you can."

"Of course."

He hesitated a moment, not seeming to be in a hurry to leave. "In fact, I'm going to be staying here on the island. This is my district, so it doesn't hurt to stay in the area for a while so I can familiarize myself with this part of the state."

"You must be new."

Gabe nodded. "Worked in Tennessee before this, but I decided I needed a change of scenery. Anyway, you said there was a dead body that you suspect might be connected with this group, correct?"

"That's right."

"I think that's worth putting some time into. And, if you need any extra manpower, I'm here."

"Sounds perfect. Thanks so much."

CHAPTER FIFTEEN

"Thanks for your help this morning," Ty told Braden as they sat on the deck with some sweet tea in hand. Country music crooned on a small speaker in the corner, and the salty scent of the ocean surrounded them. The ocean was especially angry today, and foam flew all over the shore thanks to the temperamental waves. A few puffs of the foam even stuck to the screens surrounding Ty's deck.

"Helping you is the least I can do since you're letting me stay in one of the cabanas." Braden, with his meaty muscles, had been one of the best special ops guys Ty had ever met—until a brain injury had caused his arms to tremble, at times uncontrollably. That, coupled with memory loss, had been a real struggle for Braden. Thankfully, a new doctor had straightened out his medications, and he was getting the help he needed. Having Lisa by his side had been one of his biggest blessings.

"Did Austin say you have someone coming later to check the septic?" Braden asked.

"Yeah, some new guy who moved to the island. He does septic work, so we don't have to have anyone come down from Hatteras anymore. I know I'm thankful for that." The septic had been compromised when the area flooded during the big storm last month, the same storm that had torn off a few of the roofs from his cabanas.

"We're getting all kinds of new people around here," Braden said. "And I'm glad I'm one of them."

As Ty formed his next thought, he watched more foam fly in the air and listened to the waves crashing just over the dune. "I have a question for you."

He'd been thinking about it ever since he'd visited Gilead's Cove last night—actually, since before that. Since he heard about the scars on the man's back.

"Shoot." Braden leaned back in his seat and waited, looking as if he had all the time in the world to chat.

Ty put his drink down as memories filled him. He leaned forward and licked his lips. These weren't the war stories people liked to tell. No, these stories reminded people of the depravity of the human soul. He only spoke of them when he absolutely had to.

"You were with me on that mission when we found the soldier who was being held captive," Ty started.

Braden grimaced and set his drink on the railing also. "I don't think any of us will ever forget that. His back was so raw from …"

Braden didn't finish. He didn't need to. The scene

had been horrific, and it had been a miracle the soldier had even survived what he'd endured. No human should ever have to go through that. Never.

"What about it?" Braden asked.

Ty's gaze flickered up to Braden's. "What was he whipped with? Do you remember?"

Braden's eyes widened, and he shrugged. "I don't really know. We rescued him, and we were out. I left all those details to the higher-ups. Sometimes the less we knew, the better, right? Why are you asking?"

They both had emotional scars from the battlefield. No one left situations like they'd been in unscathed, even when it appeared on the outside that they did.

"Between you and me ... that dead man who was found this week here on the island? He had scars on his back that reminded me of the soldier we rescued. I haven't been able to stop thinking about it."

Braden grunted. "You don't think it's connected, do you?"

Ty shrugged. The idea hadn't wanted to leave his thoughts. Not even right now.

He absently reached down and stroked Kujo's head as he formed his words. "I don't want to think it's connected. I mean, Iraq is a long way from Lantern Beach. But there was just something about it ..."

"What are you getting at?" Braden suddenly looked stiff and uptight. "You think someone from our war days is here on Lantern Beach torturing people? Why would someone do that? To send a message to us?"

"I don't know, Braden. The theory sounds

outlandish. I know that. I just can't shake the feeling that I have some kind of connection to this."

"If you do have a connection …" He swung his head back and forth. "I don't even know what to say, except that you should run fast. Away from here. With Cassidy. I mean, we never caught the guys responsible. They were gone when we got there. You don't think Akrum Abadi is here on Lantern Beach, do you?"

Ty shook his head, unable to imagine the terrorist leader coming here. "No, I think we'd notice that. But I … I just think there's a connection. That's all."

Braden picked up his drink again. "I'll keep my eyes open. And, if you need anything, let me know. Okay?"

Ty nodded, still feeling unsettled. "Okay. I will."

———

AFTER AGENT ABBOTT DEPARTED, Cassidy wasted no time. The pressure to find answers only grew by the moment. Cassidy could feel it. Danger was rising like the sea level in a storm.

She pulled up to the home of Rebecca Jarvis, hoping she might find some answers there.

The woman, a pretty blonde in her early thirties, answered on the first knock. She wore dress slacks and a blazer, and her hair was back in a neat twist.

Cassidy smiled when she saw her. The real estate agent had begun a campaign here on the island a couple years ago, according to local folklore. She'd decided to make life-sized cardboard cutouts of herself to place beside For Sale signs on the island.

Only, the island was known for its steady winds, and none of the signs ever stayed in place. Instead, people found them blown all over Lantern Beach.

Someone had taken it a step further and apparently began putting the stray cardboard cutouts all over town. In bathroom stalls. In the showers at rental houses. In windows.

Cassidy couldn't be sure who started it, but she suspected Wes.

The whole thing had become a running joke here on the island.

And Cassidy had to admit that it was pretty funny. She just wasn't sure Rebecca shared that humor.

"I thought I heard someone pull up," Rebecca started. "Didn't expect it to be you. Is everything okay?"

"Everything is fine. I was hoping I could ask you a few questions about a case I'm working on."

Rebecca opened the door farther. "Of course. My husband just left to go fishing, and I don't have anything scheduled for another hour. I'm showing one of the homes here on the island. It's to a tourist. They always seem to be interested until they hear the price with insurance and taxes. But it's worth it to let people see it, just in case they're one of the few who actually aren't deterred by cost."

Cassidy stepped inside the warm and cozy cottage.

Rebecca directed her to a little breakfast nook and poured her some coffee.

Cassidy didn't know the woman well, but their few exchanges had been pleasant. From what she understood, Rebecca was one of a handful of true locals left here on the island. She'd been born and raised here—and she'd stayed.

"What can I do for you?" Rebecca paused with her cup rested on her knee, one hand holding it steady.

"I need to ask you some questions about a recent real estate deal you helped with," Cassidy started.

"Of course. I'll share whatever I can—whatever I can *legally* share."

"It's about Anthony Gilead."

Rebecca's face went pale. "I see. What do you need to know?"

Cassidy rubbed the edge of her coffee cup, her eyes never leaving Rebecca. "Did the man give you any indication about why he was buying Henderson's old campground?"

"He wanted to start a spiritual retreat center. That's what he told me. It sounded like a fanatical religious group. Nothing that raised any red flags. I mean, I'm religious myself and I appreciate those freedoms—like we all should, right?"

"Did everything proceed as normal with the purchase?"

Rebecca crossed her legs and leaned back, slightly more at ease. "Yes, everything was fine. Nothing abnormal at all. I was just glad to finally sell that property. As you know, it's been an eyesore for quite a while around here."

"What was your impression of Anthony Gilead?"

She flinched, some of her ease disappearing. "He was ... he was nice. Very charismatic. The kind of person who could make you feel like you're the only one in the room."

"And you met face-to-face with him for the deal?"

"Mostly. I mean, he came here to check out the property, and he made an offer on it. He paid cash."

"What name did he use on the documents?" If Cassidy could find out the man's real name ... that would help her incredibly. Or even if she didn't know his real name, if she found out he'd signed documents using his alias, it would be Cassidy's opportunity to arrest the man.

Rebecca let out a laugh. "Oh, he didn't actually put his name on the deed. He has a board of directors, and they were on the papers. Like I said, they paid cash so it wasn't a big deal. It becomes complicated when a mortgage is involved."

"I see." Another dead-end. Disappointment bit at her. "Is there anything else he said that stands out to you?"

Rebecca tilted her head, her drink all but forgotten. "May I ask what this is about?"

"It's for a case I'm working. It's been difficult to find information on the group living behind those gates. I'm trying to cover all the angles here and learn a little more about them."

"Did they do something wrong?"

"It's really too early to say."

"Does this have to do with that dead body?"

Cassidy held back a sigh. "Again, I can't say."

Rebecca's eyes narrowed on Cassidy's. "But you're not denying it."

"Rebecca, this is an open investigation. I can't give you any details."

"I understand." She let out a sigh, as if disappointed. "But I can't really think of anything else of note. My exchanges with Anthony Gilead were pleasant and professional. I wish I could tell you more."

Cassidy set her cup on the table. "Thank you for your time, then. And if you think of anything else, please let me know."

She rose and headed toward the door. She'd so been hoping for more information. But, again, Gilead appeared to have covered his tracks.

"Chief?" Rebecca called.

Cassidy paused by the door and turned. "Yes?"

"Maybe this isn't my place, but, just in case it's important, I thought you should know …" Rebecca pressed her lips together, as if nervous. "The board of directors for Gilead's Cove just bought two other properties here on the island. And I know they want to buy more as they have the funding for it."

"More properties? What are they trying to do? Take over the whole island?"

Cassidy was halfway joking. But when she saw Rebecca's face, she had to wonder how much truth was in her question.

CHAPTER SIXTEEN

"Chief, there's someone here to see you." Melva greeted Cassidy at the front door of the station.

Cassidy was so distracted by what she'd just learned while speaking with Rebecca that she barely heard Melva. "Who's that?"

"Trisha Hartman. She's in your office."

"Trisha Hartman?" Cassidy repeated, her eyebrows furrowed together. "Thanks."

Cassidy paused for just long enough to compose herself before pushing the door to her office open and plastering on a smile. "Ms. Hartman. You made it."

Trisha looked to be in her early forties, with dark hair cut to her chin. The oversized clothing she wore did nothing to flatter her twenty-or-so pound over-weight figure. Coral-colored nails adorned each finger —except for one, which looked strangely naked beside the rest.

As Trisha stood, Cassidy noted red rims around her

eyes and dark circles beneath them. To say the woman looked tired would be an understatement. Not only did she look tired, but as she wrung her hands, she also looked nervous.

"Chief Chambers." Trisha nodded and sat back down.

Cassidy lowered herself behind her desk. "Can I get you something? Some water? Coffee?"

She shook her head. "No, I'm fine. Thank you."

Cassidy clasped her hands together in front of herself. "Thank you for coming. I know it was a long trip."

Trisha nodded. "It was. But, of course, I had to know if Al was the person you found."

"I understand it might be difficult for you to identify him, but we appreciate the fact that you're willing to try."

"Of course."

"Rather than having you look at the body itself, I have a photo to show you."

"I'm much more comfortable with that."

Cassidy pulled a glossy six-by-four from her desk and gently nudged it toward Trisha. "Is this man your husband?"

Her eyes welled with tears. "It is. That's Al. I mean, he looks a little different. But it's clearly him. Did you check for the birthmark and the scar near his appendix?"

Cassidy nodded. "I did."

A gentle sob escaped, and Trisha's hands covered

her face. "I can't believe it's him. I can't believe he's gone."

"I know this must be hard for you." Cassidy pushed a box of tissues toward her.

She raised her head, grabbed a tissue, and dabbed her eyes. "Do you have any idea who did this?"

Cassidy pressed her lips together, everything she'd learned racing through her mind. "We're working on it, but we don't know anything definitive yet."

Trisha's gaze darkened. "Was it that religious group? Did someone who's a part of that do this?"

Cassidy swallowed hard, trying to choose her words carefully. "We don't know. The group is pretty tight-lipped."

"They're the only ones I can imagine who would do this. Al probably ran out of money, so the group had no need for him anymore." She sneered.

Cassidy tilted her head. "I thought he gave all his money to you?"

"I found out yesterday that he didn't really. He only told me he did. In truth, he gave half his money to Gilead. I knew those cars were worth more than he'd told me." Bitterness edged her voice.

"How did you find that out?"

"My lawyer has been looking into his finances, that's how. There's always a paper trail."

"I'm sure that must have been hard to hear."

"Al had children he needed to take care of. They should have been his first and only obligation. Not this little organization that he claimed helped to turn his life around." Her eyes were nearly bulging, as if she couldn't contain her inner turmoil.

"I agree. That must have been difficult for you to learn."

"It was." She wiped beneath her eyes with another tissue, her emotions obviously getting the best of her. "I knew he didn't love me, but the kids ... you need to find whoever did this."

"I plan on doing just that." Cassidy paused. There was one thing Cassidy had to know before the woman left her office. "Just a final question for you, Ms. Hartman."

"Of course. Anything."

Cassidy locked gazes with her. "How was the ferry ride over this morning?"

Trisha blinked. "The ferry ride? It was fine. Why?"

"Are you sure?"

"Yes, why are you asking this?"

"Because the ferry has been closed all morning because of rough waters. Now, do you want to tell me when you really got to town, and why you lied about it?"

———

CASSIDY GLANCED at Ty as he sat across from her in the office. He'd stopped by with a late lunch—shrimp sandwiches, fruit salad, and chocolate chip cookies. She was thankful for Ty's thoughtfulness because she'd mostly forgotten to eat today and now that she thought about it, she was starving.

"So what did Trisha Hartman say?" Ty popped a grape into his mouth.

"She said she came here four days ago—"

"Which would put her on the island in time for Al's murder."

"Exactly. She said she decided to come to Lantern Beach because this was the last location where Al's phone pinged. She was worried about him and felt like they needed closure before she could move on. And her lawyer apparently had some more legal documents that Al needed to sign. But then she couldn't find him—he wasn't answering his phone. And then she heard about the body that had washed ashore."

"The timing is suspicious." Ty took another bite of his fruit salad.

"I agree. If she's telling the truth then the timing couldn't be worse."

"But there's not enough evidence to arrest her?"

Cassidy shook her head and picked one of the fried shrimp from her sandwich. "Not telling the truth doesn't mean you're a murderer. I'm going to look over the evidence from the scene one more time, though. Maybe there's something we missed that will give us a clue."

"It doesn't hurt to double-check."

Cassidy let out a long breath. "So, I need to narrow down who the killer could be—because there was someone else involved in Al's death."

"Who do you have so far?"

Her mind drifted through the possibilities. "Well, as we just talked about, his estranged wife was in town when the murder happened, yet she didn't tell me that. I had to discover it on my own. You know the spouse is always the first person we look at."

"What would she have to gain by killing him?"

"Maybe a life insurance policy. Maybe she was just angry that he walked out of her children's lives like he did. There could be any number of reasons."

"I can agree with that. What else?" Ty leaned back, fully listening and engaged.

Just one more thing to love about him. He was a great listener.

"Even though Anthony Gilead claims he's never seen Al Hartman before, all the pieces fit that Al was a part of their little group. Someone who's living at Gilead's Cove could have easily killed the man and put his body in the water to get rid of it. They were probably hoping it would wash out to sea."

"Why not just bury it? That way no one really would find it? That compound is hard to get into." Ty took a bite of his sandwich.

"That's a good question. I'm not sure."

"And Gilead seems smarter than that, you know?" Ty continued. "I'm not saying he's not responsible, but he does like to think things through. He strikes me as the type who would make someone's death look like an accident. He's not sloppy enough to make it look like a suicide while the body washes up on shore."

"I agree. But maybe one of his minions did it. Maybe they weren't as thorough." Cassidy skipped taking a bite of her sandwich. It was too messy and she had too much to say at the moment. Instead, she grabbed a chocolate chip cookie and took a bite.

Ty let out a breath. "I can't disagree with that. It's a possibility. But I'm more inclined to think that Al Hartman was a part of Gilead's Cove. I think he got the scars on his back from them, most likely. But I don't really have any solid ideas about who killed him."

Cassidy took another bite of her cookie and chewed on it a moment. "Let's say this group really is a cult and that Al was involved. If Al tried to leave or to spill information …"

"Then the leadership could be upset," Ty said. "Maybe he knew too much. But, if that was the case, Al wasn't even branded like Kaleb had been. What does that tell us?"

Cassidy shook her head, which was starting to pound. "Excellent question. I don't really know. Maybe he refused. Maybe he hadn't made it that far up the ladder. It's hard to say."

Before they could talk anymore, her phone rang.

She glanced at the screen.

It was her mom. Again.

She closed her eyes as she braced herself for the conversation.

CHAPTER SEVENTEEN

"Mom, you really shouldn't be calling," Cassidy started, her chest already squeezing with tension.

"Word about what happened to your dad is starting to leak," she said. "I need a plan."

"Why aren't you talking to the board of directors about this?" Her mom was a smart woman. This wasn't like her. Yet she always *had* been the type to put unreasonable pressure on Cassidy.

"Because the board of directors will place Fred Louis in charge. Your dad has been trying to get rid of the man for years. It's the last thing he would want. We need you. It's in the bylaws that you're next in line."

Cassidy bit down on her bottom lip before saying, "I never asked to be next in line."

"I know you didn't, but your family needs you. This is what we trained you for. You don't have to know tech to run the business."

Cassidy rubbed her temples and quickly glanced at

Ty. "I've already explained it to you, Mom. I can't leave this place. I'd be putting my life on the line. I'd live in fear every day, even with bodyguards."

"You're not living in fear there?"

She thought about her answer. She couldn't honestly tell her mother she wasn't because Cassidy was always looking over her shoulder. And she always would be. "It's different here."

"You were destined for bigger things, Cassidy. You can have and be anything you want. Yet you're on a rinky-dink island playing sheriff."

"Police chief. And what I want is to be here. This is my home now."

"I found some property here."

Cassidy paused, wondering where her mom was going with this. "Property? What are you talking about?"

"I know you're trying to set up that old cottage for retreats. But I found this house on the Puget Sound that would be perfect for Hope House. I could buy it for you. Ty could run his nonprofit from there, and he'd never have to worry about money again. It would solve any financial issues you might be having. You could have everything you want, only here, close to us."

"But that's not where … we're in the center of all things military here in this area. It's an easy drive from Norfolk or Fayetteville. This is where we need to be." Cassidy didn't want to explain everything to her mom. She didn't have to, for that matter. Yet she sensed a vulnerability to her mom's words.

"I know you don't think money is important. But with money, you can accomplish a lot of good things. You can make an impact on the world. You can get the justice you're seeking without being on the police force. You can start your own national organization. All you have to do is come back here."

She pressed her eyes shut. "I can't, Mom. I just can't."

"Think about it one more day. I'm going to hold off the board the best I can. But please consider this possibility. It would mean a lot to our family. Blood is important. Maybe it's the most important thing."

As Cassidy hung up, she glanced over at Ty then filled him in on the conversation.

"Wow, she really pulled out all the tricks, didn't she?" Ty offered a compassionate frown.

"Yeah, she really did." A heaviness pressed on Cassidy. She hated to let her family down, to not be there for them when they needed her. But she couldn't return to Seattle for so many reasons.

"Can you really see yourself staying here forever, Cassidy?"

Ty's words startled her. "What do you mean? We talked about this before we got married. Wherever you are, that's where I want to be."

"And that's what I want also. It's just that … "

"It's just that what?" She braced herself for wherever this conversation might go.

"It's just that … I keep worrying that they're going to find you here. DH-7. I know they disbanded, but neither of us is stupid enough to think there aren't die-hard stragglers out there."

"That may be true, but they could find me anywhere …"

"I also worry that …" Tension stretched through his words.

She reached forward and grabbed his hand. "What is it, Ty?"

There was clearly something he wasn't saying.

He swallowed so hard that she could see his throat muscles tightening. "I know I'm going to sound crazy, but I can't stop thinking that someone from my past might have followed me here to the island."

She had no idea what he was talking about. "What do you mean by 'someone from my past'?"

He shrugged, his gaze still heavy. "I mean … we were just theorizing about what happened to Al. I can't help but think that whoever tortured him might in some way be connected with me. With my past as a SEAL."

"You think you have something to do with this man's murder? Unofficially, of course." Cassidy couldn't believe she was saying the words.

"I don't know. I can't shake the feeling that we're being watched. I can't shake the feeling that I'm somehow connected with Al. And I can't stand the thought that I might be putting you in danger."

She squeezed his hand. "Don't talk like that. Of course you're not putting me in danger."

"Well, not on purpose, of course. But what if something in my past is making it unsafe for you to be around me?" His tortured gaze met hers.

"Are you suggesting that I should move to Seattle, Ty?" Cassidy couldn't believe that question had even left her lips. The words made her feel sick to her stomach.

"Not exactly. It's just that we both need to be open to whatever the future brings. If you being here and around me could hurt you, then we need to evaluate."

"Evaluate what? Us?" Her voice rose with concern.

Ty stood and stepped closer, his hand going to her waist. "No, never us, Cassidy."

"Then what?" Everything nearly felt like it was spinning around her.

"Then we have to evaluate our situation."

Her hand skimmed the edge of his jaw. "Your dream is to be here, Ty. This is what you've worked so hard to do. I don't want to put that in jeopardy."

"I know you don't." He gently cupped her face. "Whatever happens, we're in this together, right?"

She nodded. "Of course. Together. Forever."

Then why did Cassidy feel like they were facing a potential crack in the road up ahead—a crack that might easily divide them?

———

AFTER TY LEFT, Cassidy called Dane and officially extended a contract to him to work for the island's police department. He accepted on the spot and said he would come in the next morning to begin training.

At least one thing was going according to plan.

As Cassidy chewed on her thoughts regarding the rest of the day, Mac stepped into her office.

"Are you done with boot camp for the day?" Cassidy asked as he took a seat across from her.

"Done for today, and only one more day to go."

"And what will you do next?"

"Don't worry, I'll keep looking for trouble." He grinned and wagged his eyebrows before shifting. "I heard something today that I thought I would share."

"Please do."

"I was down at the hardware store when I overheard a conversation. Apparently, there was some conflict between one of our locals and our dead guy."

Mac had her full attention now. "Which local would that be?"

"Rebecca, our town real estate agent."

Cassidy sucked in a breath. She hadn't seen that one coming, and Rebecca certainly hadn't mentioned anything about it. "Any details on their topic of conversation?"

"Nope, just that it was heated."

"It looks like I need to go pay her another visit."

Mac cocked his head to the side. "Mind if I come along?"

"Not at all."

Ten minutes later, they pulled up to Rebecca's house.

Her eyes narrowed with confusion when she opened the front door. "Hello, Mac, Chief Chambers. I didn't expect to see you again. Especially not so soon."

Cassidy frowned. She hadn't expected to be here again so soon either. "We need to talk."

"Of course. Come in." Rebecca opened the door wider, and the scent of seafood circled them. "It's whitefish stew. An old family recipe. If you want to stick around thirty minutes, you can have some."

"Thanks, but that's okay." Cassidy noted that Rebecca's professional outfit was gone, and in its place she wore an old stained shirt and jeans. Had the woman just gotten comfortable in some old clothes after a long day at work? Or was her image of being a successful realtor a façade she put on with her business suit?

Cassidy and Mac stepped inside but didn't bother to sit. No, Cassidy wanted to get right to the heart of the matter.

"Rebecca, someone in town saw you arguing with our victim last week."

Her face visibly paled. "Did they?"

"You need to tell me what's going on."

"I didn't kill him." Her voice wavered as her gaze bobbed back and forth between Cassidy and Mac.

"I didn't say you killed him," Cassidy said. "But I am saying that you're withholding information."

"I knew how it would look. And my husband and I depend on my income to make a living. He's been out of work for the past fourteen months because of a back injury."

"I'm not trying to start trouble," Cassidy said. "I'm only trying to solve a potential murder."

Rebecca cast her gaze to the floor and shook her head. "The dead man cornered me at the general store last week. I didn't know his name, or I would have come forward with it."

The jury was still out on that one. "Had you met him before?"

"No, I hadn't. Frankly, I couldn't believe he knew who I was. But he looked stressed. Really stressed. Sweat poured down his face, and he could hardly get a deep breath."

Cassidy and Mac exchanged a look before Cassidy asked, "What did he want to talk to you about?"

"I told you that the group over at Gilead's Cove bought up two more homes on the island. Well, the closing on those houses just went through last week. He asked me to stop the deal."

Cassidy narrowed her eyes as she processed the information. "Would you even be able to do that?"

She shrugged. "I suppose I could have stepped away as the agent for the deal. It might have slowed things up. But, really, all that would have accomplished was me not getting my commission. They would have still found a way to buy the property, even if it was delayed."

"Why did he want you to stop the deal?" Mac asked.

"He wouldn't give me any details. He only said it would be a mistake."

Cassidy waited for more, but Rebecca remained quiet. "Nothing else?"

Rebecca shook her head. "No, nothing. I asked for more information, wondering if his proposition was something I should consider. But this guy couldn't give me any concrete or moral reason why the deal shouldn't go through."

"Did he give you any indication if he was affiliated with the group from Gilead's Cove?" Mac asked.

"No, he didn't. He wasn't one of the names on the board of directors for Gilead. But he looked scared."

"And this was last week?" Potentially only days before he died. The bad feeling churned harder in Cassidy's stomach.

"That's right." Rebecca wrapped her arms across her chest, her eyes wide with anxiety. "I promise I didn't kill him. I had no reason to. I have other things to worry about, things more important than stopping someone from buying up land on the island. I'm just trying to make a living and put groceries on the table."

"One more question," Cassidy said. "Do you have any idea where Al was staying here on the island?"

If he wasn't staying at Gilead's Cove—and that was still a possibility—then where had he called home?

"I have no idea. But, if it will help, I can check with my company's rental records. Maybe he was utilizing our off-season rates."

"Please do check that. I'd appreciate it." In the meantime, Cassidy would be checking with the other rental companies in the area as well.

CHAPTER EIGHTEEN

Anxiety knotted in Moriah's stomach as she pulled on a clean tunic the next morning.

She'd been summoned.

By Gilead.

And she had no idea what that meant.

Did he meet with everyone who came here? Had he found out Moriah had taken that loaf of bread?

Fear spread through her at the thought.

Moriah smoothed her tunic and paused. She wished she had a mirror, so she could check her hair. Or maybe even some makeup.

Outward appearance wasn't important. She knew that. Still, she'd like to look presentable for the meeting. Gilead always looked so well put-together.

"Why do you look so nervous?" Ruth paused as she climbed out of the bed on the other side of the RV. Just last night, they'd been paired as roommates.

Moriah actually preferred to live alone, but beggars

couldn't be choosers, as the saying went. Still, her extra loaf of bread was in a cubby she'd found beneath her own bed. She hoped Ruth didn't get nosy and find out —or catch her eating it.

Moriah shoved the thoughts aside and turned to her roommate. "I just don't know what to expect."

"I'm sure it will be fine." Ruth lumbered to the sink and started the water to wash her face.

The woman was big-boned, and her personality seemed as strong as her features. She wasn't the type of person Moriah would normally be friends with. Ruth's opinions were too strong and unyielding for Moriah's tastes. But Moriah could learn to get along with all kinds of people. It was the way of Gilead.

"How has the protocol been going this week?" Ruth asked.

The protocol was what they called the personal development plan each person received. Moriah was at the beginning of this plan. Hers was a time of learning and serving right now.

Moriah leaned against the kitchen cabinet. She still had a few minutes until she had to leave. "It's been … it's been great. I've worked during the morning. I've had my therapy sessions during the afternoon."

Ruth towel-dried her face and turned to her. "Have you opened up your mind to the possibilities of what it would be like to belong?"

Warmth filled Moriah's chest. "I've never felt like I've belonged this much. I've always been the outcast, but here …"

Ruth smiled. "You feel like you're one of us."

"Yes, that's right. Exactly."

Ruth folded her towel and placed it on the small counter. "Then perhaps Gilead is meeting with you to discuss the next step."

"What do you mean?" The next step? Moriah had barely been able to comprehend everything she'd already learned. She hadn't been prepped yet about what would happen next.

"There are levels of trust and community here. You're new and just beginning this journey. But there are opportunities to advance. And, of course, before you can do that, you'll have to show your complete loyalty to us by going through an initiation process. It's really a beautiful thing."

Initiation? The last time Moriah had heard that word, she'd been lured into a sorority—only none of it was real. She'd acted like a servant to those girls for two weeks before they'd proclaimed it was all a joke and had a good laugh on her account.

Moriah cleared her throat, trying to shove aside the memories. That was what Gilead would tell her to do. "What happens there?"

Ruth smiled again and began to brush her long, dark hair. "I can't tell you. It's a surprise. But I will say, this is awfully fast for that to happen. Unless you've really caught Gilead's eye."

"We've barely spoken. In fact, I have trouble looking at him. I feel so small when I'm around him."

"Remember, we're all equal here. There are no small people."

"Moriah?" a deep voice called from outside her RV.

She cracked the door open and saw Dietrich waiting there. "Yes?"

"Gilead requests to see you now."

"Yes, sir." She rubbed her hands against her clothes and lowered her gaze as she stepped outside and followed Dietrich down the gravel road. She asked no questions.

Inside the meeting center, they went upstairs. Dietrich opened a door and stretched his arm to indicate she should go inside one of the rooms.

Her pulse raced again. She'd never been up here. Never been into Gilead's office. Never even spoken one-on-one with this man.

What if he'd discovered that she'd taken food? Would he kick her out? Was that what this was about? Would she be given punishment?

She knew she shouldn't have taken the bread. Yet she'd been so hungry. And she found comfort in knowing she could nibble on the loaf whenever the pangs hit her.

Gilead smiled at her from the other side of his desk and rose. "Ms. Roberts. Thank you for meeting with me. Please, have a seat."

He indicated she should sit in one of the chairs against the wall. To her surprise, he crossed from around his desk and sat beside her.

The man was so handsome. Moriah knew it was

wrong to think that way of a leader. But his eyes were so blue that she wanted to stare at them. And his hair was a thick brown, his build lean, and his smile contagious.

She might have even daydreamed about the man a few times.

But she'd asked for forgiveness afterward. It seemed disrespectful.

"I wanted to see how your stay here has been so far." Gilead leaned his elbow on the arm of the chair, his full attention on her.

Moriah's fingers nervously wound together in her lap. "It's been great. Thank you so much for welcoming me here. Gilead's Cove has been an answer to prayer."

His smile widened. "I'm glad to hear that. That's what we're here for. So many people in this world today are lost and feel alone. We were never meant to live life that way. First Corinthians 1:10 tells us 'in the name of our Lord Jesus Christ, that all of you agree with one another in what you say and that there be no divisions among you, but that you be perfectly united in mind and thought.'"

"I'm so glad that God has given you a word on this."

"It's all in the Bible. But we get blinders on. We see life and the Bible through the lenses we've been taught to see it from. I like to come at it with no preconceived notions. And that's the gift that God has given."

"Yes, sir. And what a wonderful gift."

She could feel his gaze studying her and didn't

know whether she should feel delighted or scared. She wavered somewhere between the two.

"I'm sure you're curious about why I wanted to see you," he said.

"Yes, sir."

"Elizabeth tells me you're making good progress here. She said your sessions together have shown tremendous growth."

"I hope so. I feel like I've grown so much, even in such a short time."

"I see something special in you, Moriah." He reached forward and rested his hand on her wrist. "I think you're going to do great things here."

Moriah's cheeks flushed. No one had ever thought she would do great things. No one. Not even her parents. "I'm honored."

"It's too soon for an official ceremony to bring you in as a shepherd. But you're well on your way. I wanted to tell you to keep up the good work."

"Yes, sir. I will." Her cheeks flushed again as Gilead continued to stare at her.

"And you don't have to call me sir. Call me Gilead."

"Yes, sir—I mean, yes, Gilead."

He grinned and stood. She instantly missed the warmth of his touch as he released her wrist.

For the first time in a long time, she felt like someone actually could see past the mess of her life and into her soul. She felt like someone understood her. Saw potential in her.

Delight filled her at the thought.

Coming here had been the right choice. Now she knew that for certain. It was worth it, even with her empty belly and cold arms. Even though she missed her parents and her beautiful West Virginia.

She stepped toward the door, but Gilead's voice stopped her. She paused to turn, only to find he was standing close—much closer than she'd anticipated.

She glanced up at him. At the blue eyes that probed into hers. Gilead made her feel safe and welcome and worthy.

How could one man have that much power over her in such a short amount of time?

To her surprise, his hand brushed her cheek. Something crackled between them—some kind of tension.

"I have big plans for you," he murmured, his eyes swirling with an unreadable emotion. "Big plans."

Big plans? What was he talking about? She had no idea.

But she couldn't wait to find out.

CHAPTER NINETEEN

After a vigorous early morning run, Cassidy and Ty were drinking coffee on the deck while Kujo lay at their feet. The sun had risen, but the color of the sky was still pastel and calming, the sight promising a new day.

As she'd jogged, Cassidy had kept her eyes open for that man she'd seen on the dune a couple days ago, but he'd been strangely absent. Maybe his presence wasn't significant. But at this point in her investigation, she wasn't discounting anything.

The sound of a vehicle pulling down the gravel lane filled the air. A moment later, a door slammed, footsteps pounded up the stairs, and Wes appeared on the deck.

"Sorry to drop by unannounced." Wes leaned down to pat Kujo's head. "I dropped my phone and the screen shattered. Otherwise, I would have called."

"Everything okay?" Ty tensed beside her, his instincts kicking in. "You sound urgent."

Wes's gaze went to Cassidy. "It's actually about Gilead's Cove."

"Anything you know about them, I'm all ears." She straightened and put her coffee down on the railing beside her.

She'd hardly been able to sleep last night as she'd contemplated the case. She wouldn't be able to rest until she knew exactly what was going on behind that fence. That community was a part of the island here, and it was her job to keep the island safe. To keep everyone on the island safe—even the people who'd willingly chosen to live in that compound.

The more she learned about them, the less comfortable she felt.

"My friend up in Nags Head is headed there today," Wes said. "He'll arrive in about three hours, to be exact. They hired him to install some solar panels."

Cassidy's pulse spiked. "Is that right?"

"Yeah, he called to ask me about the place. For the record, I dropped my phone after he called. I leaned over the deck railing to talk to my neighbor, and the phone fell from my pocket. Anyway, apparently this solar panel order is pretty large, and the man he spoke with said they're trying to be a self-sustaining community."

That made sense. There was less government interference and regulation that way.

"Good to know." Cassidy's thoughts raced ahead, the start of a plan forming in her mind. "Does your friend need some help?"

Wes squinted. "What do you mean?"

"I mean, does he need some additional manpower? I've been trying to get into that compound to find out more information. They're not willingly going to let me poke around. This might be the perfect opportunity."

"But they would recognize you." Ty visibly tensed as he turned toward her. "That would never work."

"I know. I can't go myself." Her thoughts continued to circle.

"Then who would go?" Ty asked.

Cassidy nibbled on her bottom lip a moment, various scenarios playing out in her mind. "I'm sure Gilead has already scoped out most people here on the island. But he probably doesn't know about Dane yet."

"Who's Dane?" Wes squinted with confusion.

"He's my newest officer. He's just starting today."

"And you want to throw him into this?" Ty asked, his voice tinged with doubt. "Is that a good idea?"

"Dane has had a lot of experience—not here, but in Cincinnati. He has the know-how to handle this. I hate to throw him into something like this on his first day too. Then again, I'm not sure I have any other choice." She glanced at Wes. "Do you think your friend would be up for something like this?"

Wes nodded. "I'd be happy to ask him … but I'm going to have to borrow your phone."

———

CASSIDY STEPPED into her office and released a long breath.

The wheels had been set in motion, and in two hours Dane should be inside Gilead's Cove. Every bit of information they could gather about the place would help their investigation. She just prayed everyone would stay safe. She'd never forgive herself if something happened on her watch.

At the moment, Dane was filling out a pile of paperwork to make his job here official.

She paused in her doorway and glanced around her office, some kind of internal warning sounding in her mind.

What felt different in here? She couldn't pinpoint what it was—maybe just gut instinct.

But she didn't like the feeling.

She scanned the surroundings again. Her file drawers were closed. Her chair was pushed beneath her desk. The trashcan was in place.

Her perusal stopped at the crime board behind her desk.

One of the pictures was crooked, she realized. That must be it. Maybe the magnet had slipped or something. But it was nothing criminal.

Cassidy nearly laughed at herself for being so paranoid.

Instead, she slipped behind her desk. But no sooner had she done that then Melva appeared at her door, wringing her hands together.

"Chief, someone else is here to see you," Melva said.

"This is a bad time." Cassidy still had to review the notes she'd made for Dane and sign some of the papers.

"They said it's important."

Cassidy drew in a long breath. This sleepy town was suddenly feeling very needy and demanding. "Pertaining to …?"

"They said their daughter is missing. They think she came here."

And Cassidy had thought a job on Lantern Beach would be easy. She couldn't be more wrong. "Send them in."

A moment later, a man and woman in their fifties came into her office. Both were overweight, and their features looked drawn with tension. They introduced themselves as Mr. and Mrs. Cross.

After getting them coffee, Cassidy sat down to chat. "What can I do for you?"

They exchanged a glance before the woman spoke up. "We think our daughter came here to Lantern Beach, and we're worried about her."

"Why do you think she came here? Could you start from the beginning?"

"Our daughter has always been a bit of a lost soul," Mrs. Cross started. "She's a beautiful girl, but her self-esteem has always been low. She suffered with depression, and that led her to make some bad choices—choices like drugs and bad relationships."

"Okay." The story wasn't an entirely unfamiliar one. Just last month, Cassidy had tracked down a runaway teen on the island. Some people came here because they thought the ocean could fix everything. If only that were true …

"About a month ago, we noticed some changes in her," the father continued, his voice grim as his wife gripped his hand. "She'd met someone new."

"A romantic interest?"

"No, we don't think so." Mrs. Cross shook her head. "But someone was coming through town and leading these … these … revivals. A friend invited her and she went. She came home and looked hopeful for the first time in a long time."

Revivals? The breath left Cassidy's lungs.

"At first, we thought it was a good thing," Mr. Cross said, his features still drawn. "I mean, we're not opposed to religion. We're Christians ourselves, and we believe in the good Lord above. But something about this was different. She sold all of her possessions—not that she had much. And then she packed up and said she was going to leave to live at a retreat center affiliated with this group."

"We couldn't talk her out of it," Mrs. Cross continued. "She was convinced if she joined this movement that she was going to find a new life for herself. But now we haven't been able to get in contact with her. We're worried."

"I can understand that," Cassidy said. "Did she tell you she was coming here?"

Mrs. Cross squirmed. "No, not exactly. But we tracked her cell phone—not as a means of being controlling. But it's good to know where the people you love are. You never know what could happen . . . anyway, the phone last pinged here. And then it went dead. There's nothing."

"I see." Cassidy would guess their daughter may have had to turn it over as a stipulation of staying at Gilead's Cove. It fit what she knew so far about the group.

Mr. Cross shifted. "There's one other thing. Our daughter was married—divorced, actually. She'd moved back in with us until she could get back on her feet. She didn't have a good marriage—not at all. Her husband was ten years older and very controlling, to say the least. He was just one of her many problems. Men ... they've always been our daughter's weakness."

Mr. and Mrs. Cross glanced at each other again, a worried look passing between them.

"Two days after she left, the police found him dead," Mrs. Cross said.

Cassidy sucked in a breath. "Do they think your daughter killed him?"

"No, we don't think so. But the way he was killed ..." The father's voice faded.

"How was he killed?" Cassidy could hardly breathe as she waited for their response.

"He had these marks on his back, like he was tortured. But, ultimately, the police told us he was strangled. With a rope."

Cassidy's mind raced at the similarities between that man and Al Hartman. Maybe this was her first real lead.

"What's your daughter's name?"

"Her name is Moriah," Mrs. Cross said. "Moriah Roberts. Please help us find her. Please."

———

CASSIDY HAD PROMISED Mr. and Mrs. Cross that she would do her best to locate their daughter. They'd given her a picture, and—Cassidy couldn't be certain—but the pretty girl in the photo had almost looked like the woman Cassidy had seen cleaning the bathroom at the compound.

Hopefully, she'd figure out some answers soon. In the meantime, the Crosses had left, and now Cassidy had to get ready for Dane's undercover assignment. She didn't have much time. Wes's friend and three members of his crew were on their way, and she needed to continue to fill Dane in on everything going on.

He sat in his new office looking over the case files now. Mac stayed with him, briefing him on the area's dynamics. It was the best Cassidy could do being short-staffed.

She glanced at her watch.

She only had an hour, and there was so much she needed to do.

But before she dove into her to-do list, she picked up her phone and called the Lansing, West Virginia, Police Department. She was put through to a Detective Torres and introduced herself.

"I'm investigating a potential murder here in

Lantern Beach, and I understand there was a similar one in your town," she stated.

She ran through what she knew and how she'd found out about Vince Roberts. The detective listened as she spoke, grunting on occasion, but not saying anything until Cassidy finished.

"I'd say it definitely sounds like there could be some similarities," Detective Torres said. "But there's one problem."

"What's that?"

"We already caught Vince's killer."

Cassidy nibbled on the inside of her mouth. That fact didn't fit the theories that had been forming in the back of her mind, and now she needed to backtrack. "Did you? And this person has been charged? Did he confess?"

"Yes, he was another drug dealer, someone Moriah used to hang out with. He said he did it."

"And there was evidence to support his confession?" This *definitely* didn't fit the pieces of what Cassidy knew. No, that meant this killer would have been behind bars when Al had died.

"Yes, there was evidence," Torres said. "There was also flakka in his system."

Cassidy sucked in a deep breath at the mention. "Flakka?"

"Yes, I take it you're familiar with the drug?"

Cassidy could hardly breathe. Flakka was the drug DH-7 was known for. It was their signature—a psychotic, hallucinogenic drug that made people act crazy. "Yes, I'm familiar with it."

"Most parts of the country have an opioid crisis. Here in our county, it's flakka. People have gone crazy with the drug in the past three months."

Everything went still around Cassidy. "Any idea why?"

"We're not sure, but we strongly suspect the drug has ties with a religious group that passed through. They were quite the hit here, especially in our poorer communities. Apparently, they gave anyone wanting to join them the opportunity for a fresh start in a place where they wouldn't have to worry about money anymore."

"And this drug was a part of their program?"

"As far as we can tell, it wasn't official. But some of the leaders used it and shared it with a few in town. That was all it took to set the ball in motion, as they say."

"What's the name of that group?"

"I don't know if they had an official name, but I believe their leader is a man named Anthony Gilead."

CHAPTER TWENTY

When Cassidy stepped out of her office, she spotted Dane emerging from his office with Mac. He'd been transformed from a newly minted officer into a solar panel installer, complete with dark-blue Dickies jeans, a light-blue button-up shirt with the name "Hank" embroidered on the pocket, plastic-framed glasses, and a fake mustache.

"You sure you're okay with doing this?" Cassidy paused in front of him and studied his disguise. Mac had done a good job.

Dane brushed off his shirt. "I've got this. My only goal is to gather information and make observations. I can handle that—even if it is my first day on the job."

"If in doubt, talk about off-grid living, free-range chickens, and pour-over coffee," Mac said. "I saw that on a YouTube video. The new brand of hippies love stuff like that. Peace, love, and embracing a complicated simplicity."

"One more thing." Cassidy held up her phone. "Can you keep your eyes open for this girl?"

Dane took her phone and examined the picture there. "Sure thing. Can I ask who she is?"

"Her name is Moriah Roberts. She disappeared from West Virginia earlier this week, and her parents are worried. Her husband also turned up dead. I'd like to know if she's living in the compound or not."

This woman could be a connection between two dead men. Was she a suspect? Cassidy didn't know— especially since someone else had confessed to the first murder. But she was definitely a person of interest.

"Will do."

"I'll be parked the next street over. No one should see me there, but I'll be close in case you need me. All you have to do is call."

"I will." Dane squinted. "I can handle this, Chief. I promise."

She nodded, still uneasy. "I know you can. Thanks."

Just then, Wes's friend pulled up behind the building, as Cassidy had directed. She saw the van from her office window. With a final nod, Dane stepped out the back door and jumped into the work van with him.

Cassidy's heart still pounded furiously as she watched them pull away.

"It's going to be okay, Cassidy," Mac said.

"I know. I'm just on edge." She reached for the keys in her pocket, but she must have left them in her office.

As she stepped that way, Mac called out behind her. "I'm going to go with you."

"You don't have to do that."

"I insist. Besides, I promised Ty."

Ty was busy meeting with the septic guy today or, no doubt, he'd be here himself.

"That's fine, then," Cassidy said. "I just need my keys."

She went to her desk drawer and opened it. No keys.

Where else might she have left them?

Cassidy sat down and tried to run through her morning. It had been frantic with the addition of training Dane, having him go undercover, and Moriah's parents showing up.

She glanced at the floor and saw a glimmer there.

Her keys. They must have fallen from her pocket.

As she pulled herself back to an upright position, something beneath the desk caught her eye. She frowned as she reached for it.

"What's that you have there?" Mac appeared in the doorway.

She put a finger over her lips as she examined the object. Cassidy couldn't be completely sure, but it looked like a listening device had been planted in her office.

———

"WHO COULD HAVE PLANTED a bug in your office?" Mac asked, once they were in Cassidy's car and sitting on a side road near the Gilead's Cove compound.

They'd put the device in a plastic bag and stored it in the safe at the police station. No one would hear anything in there. When Cassidy got back to the office, she would send the listening device off to be tested. Maybe there were prints on it.

They'd also swept the rest of the office and Cassidy's SUV, just to be safe. Both were clear.

But that did little to put Cassidy at ease.

"That's a great question." And one that Cassidy hadn't stopped thinking about. She had no idea who would have planted that device or how they would have done it without her noticing.

"Let's start with the obvious." Mac leaned back in his seat, his gaze fixated on the fence to Gilead's Cove in the distance. The van had gone in fifteen minutes ago, and there'd been no sign of movement since then. "Who's been in your office over the past couple days— assuming that's when it was left there."

It was true. For all they knew, it could have been there for longer.

Cassidy settled back also and took a sip of her coffee. She reminded herself not to drink too much— there were no bathroom breaks allowed during stake-outs. "Let's see. I had Trisha Hartman, our dead man's wife. I've had Dane. Ty. Melva. Leggott. Today I had Moriah's parents. Can I see any of them leaving a listening device? Absolutely not."

"Who else could have gotten into your office? Maybe after hours."

"I keep it locked up. But this morning, I did think

something felt different, though. I figured the heat had turned on and ruffled some of my papers and pictures."

Mac grunted and reached into a paper bag to grab some popcorn. As Cassidy watched him a minute, she couldn't help but muse that the man looked like he was settling back to watch his favorite action movie.

"I'll ask Leggott if he let anyone in after hours and didn't keep an eye on them." Cassidy stole one of the buttery kernels, unable to resist the tantalizing smell. If it had been kettle corn, she would have snatched the entire bag. "And I'll also get Melva to check the security footage."

"Then the second question is this: *why* would someone leave a listening device?"

Cassidy stared across the field at the compound. "My only guess would be because of Gilead's Cove. It's the only big thing I'm working right now."

"Or could it be because … of your past?" His voice trailed off.

Cassidy licked her lips. She wanted to deny it. To tell Mac there was no way that was true.

But her mom had called her twice this week. If someone was monitoring her mom's line, then the call could have led them to Cassidy.

And then there was the flakka in West Virginia. Was that just a coincidence? The drug had been growing in popularity. But since DH-7 had disbanded, authorities hoped the growth would subside.

Cassidy had to play it safe here.

Then again, what if Al Hartman's death wasn't

connected with Gilead's Cove at all? What if she'd been looking in the wrong direction? She didn't think that was the case, but she needed to be openminded.

"Cassidy?"

She turned toward Mac and sighed. "To be honest, I just don't know. I don't want to be narrow-minded here and not see something that I should."

"You're doing fine. I know there's a lot going on right now." He shifted. "My other question is, was there anything that whoever planted that device might have heard that you didn't want them to?"

That was a great question. "I haven't had any conversations about my past, if that's what you're getting at. Other than that, I have talked to Moriah's parents. Trisha Hartman. And Dane." She startled. "What if Dane is in danger? What if they know he's a cop?"

"Let's slow down a little. They shouldn't have any reason to feel threatened by him. Plus, they're sending in a crew of four men, right? Just because someone was listening doesn't mean they could pick Dane out of a lineup. He'll call if he needs us."

"You're right. I'm overthinking it here. There's just so much on the line ... I want to keep this town safe, Mac."

"And you're doing a fine job. Just don't let the pressure get to you."

"I'm trying not to. I really am."

Music cut through the air. Cassidy turned and saw Serena heading down the road in Elsa. Why in the world was the girl coming down an empty road with no houses?

Serena slowed near Cassidy and stuck her head out the window. Her music—"Eye of the Tiger" was the current song—still blared and caused unnecessary attention on them.

Begrudgingly, Cassidy lowered her window. She wasn't in the mood for chitchat right now. "You've got to turn the music off."

Serena's eyes widened. "Oh, you're doing police-y kind of things?"

"Yes, please—turn it off. Now."

Serena reached inside and the music went silent.

Cassidy breathed in and out, trying to keep her patience. Finally, she turned to Serena, attempting to subdue the irritation in her voice as she asked, "How's it going?"

"Not many people buying ice cream today."

"It is only forty-two degrees and only locals." Maybe Serena would do better if she sold coffee instead. Cassidy would be a regular customer.

"I know. But I could really use the extra cash. How do people survive here on the island this time of year?"

"I thought you were writing for the newspaper," Mac said.

"I was. But then I got a few details wrong in that article about fishing policies, and now Ernestine said I need to take a break."

"You mean because you told people regulations had

changed and surf fishing wasn't legal anymore?" Mac said.

Serena shrugged. "It was a misunderstanding."

"We almost had a mutiny here in the town because of it," Mac said.

Serena leaned out the window, unaffected by the words. "Did I tell you I signed up to take some online classes so I can finish my degree?"

"No, I hadn't heard," Cassidy said. "It sounds like a smart idea."

"That's what Aunt Skye said also. Oh, and guess what?" A grin stretched across her face. "Dietrich asked me out."

"Did he? I guess that means he's going to be in town for a while?"

She nodded. "Yeah, he said he was moving here to Lantern Beach permanently. Can you believe it, Cassidy?"

"And what is this Dietrich guy going to do here permanently?"

"He wants to start a charter fishing business. I can't wait for you to meet him. He's such a great guy. And he's handsome to boot. Did I mention that?"

"That's really great, Serena."

She beamed. "I think so too. Anyway, I better get back to work. I have to sell at least ten things to break even and pay for gas."

"How many have you sold so far?" Cassidy asked.

"None." She shrugged.

Frowning, Cassidy reached into her wallet. "You

convinced me. Mac and I will take ice cream sandwiches."

Serena's eyes lit. "And how about one of my shirts I designed just for Lantern Beach?"

Cassidy let her head fall to the side and gave her a look. "Not today. Maybe next time."

"I'll remember that."

"I know you will." Right now, Cassidy just needed to focus … and eat her ice cream sandwich.

CHAPTER TWENTY-ONE

The solar panel crew was on the compound for only two hours—long enough to measure and give an estimate, apparently. The work van dropped Dane off at the general store, where Cassidy and Mac picked him up.

She didn't wait until she got back to the station to probe Dane. She wanted to know what her newest officer had found out now. "Anything?"

"The place gives me the creeps," Dane started, peeling off his fake mustache. "No one makes eye contact. And the leader … he's a piece of work."

Cassidy couldn't agree more. "I know you weren't able to investigate much but … anything of note?"

Dane stared out the window and pulled off his glasses, rubbing the bridge of his nose. "There was one man stationed to oversee us. I asked him a few questions, trying to sound casual, like if he was ever able to leave the Cove and explore the rest of the island."

"And he said?" Mac asked.

"He said, 'Why would I want to do that when I have everything here?'"

Cassidy shivered again and continued to drive back toward the station. "Did you see any possible ways we can breach the area to find out more information?"

Dane leaned forward, toward the front seat. "No, not really. I mean, the property goes right up to the sound, but there's someone patrolling that area. I doubt you could get past. And there aren't many trees on the property itself. However, there are some woods that back up to the edge of the property on the north side."

"That's good to know," Mac said. "It could prove helpful."

"And I saw a woman walking toward the woods. She was … staring longingly at the area, if you ask me. I know that sounds dramatic, but … anyway. It was kind of strange. Who knows but maybe that's a routine? Maybe someone could catch her there one day."

Cassidy nodded. The observation was a good one. "It's something to think about, at least."

"And I have the feeling they have a schedule there," Dane continued. "From what I gathered, everyone eats breakfast, lunch, and dinner together. They have seminars and meetings in between. Everyone appears to have been assigned chores as well."

"Sounds like a well-oiled machine," Cassidy said. "Did you hear any names, by chance?"

Dane shrugged and stared ahead in thought again. "Anthony Gilead, obviously. There was a man named

Barnabas. Another named Kaleb. And I heard someone mention something about a Dietrich."

Cassidy sucked in a breath. Dietrich? Could that be the same Dietrich that Serena was talking about?

Serena … she was just the type to get pulled into something like this.

Cassidy had to warn Serena to stay away. And she had to pray that the girl would listen to her. Infatuation could be a powerful thing… and that scared Cassidy.

Her phone rang. It was the real estate and management company Rebecca worked for. Rebecca had instructed one of the property managers to call Cassidy. He'd found a listing for an Al Hartman, and he was heading over to the house now if Cassidy wanted to take a look inside.

———

CASSIDY DROPPED Dane back at the station to finish some paperwork. Then she and Mac headed to the rental house.

It wasn't one of the large, oceanfront houses that some people rented. No, the humble cottage probably had less than a thousand square feet.

Her feelings remained conflicted about this Al guy. Was he a member of Gilead's Cove? If so, did that mean not everyone stayed in the gated community?

And how about Dietrich? He wasn't staying in the community either.

The bad feeling in Cassidy's gut continued to grow with every new fact she learned.

Maybe she'd find some answers inside.

An apprehensive-looking man named Paul Richards met them on the driveway. Cassidy and Ty had seen him at church a couple times, but the two had never really spoken with him. He offered a tight smile before punching in a code on the door and opening it.

"This is the house Rebecca said you were inquiring about," Paul said. "It's usually a vacation rental, but Mr. Hartman asked if he could do a short-term rental of three months."

"Did he say anything else?" Cassidy asked, pausing by the front door and tugging her jacket closer as a cool wind bulldozed this side of the house.

"He said he was from West Virginia. He was here to start fresh. He seemed like a pretty normal guy. Nothing raised any warning bells."

"Good to know." Cassidy gave him a nod. "I'm going to check out the inside. You may want to stay here. I'm not sure what we're going to find."

In all likelihood, it could be a crime scene.

Paul didn't argue. "Actually, if it's okay with you, I'm renovating the kitchen at home. My wife would love for me to finish it. Are you good here? Just lock up when you leave?"

Cassidy nodded. "We are. We can always call if we need you."

Apprehension filled Cassidy as she took the first

step into the house. She scanned everything around her. The layout was typical for homes in this area, with one large great room complete with kitchen, dining room, and living room. A hallway stretched beyond that, and, most likely, Cassidy would find three bedrooms and a bathroom there.

Carefully, Cassidy walked through the front rooms. She saw nothing—no sign that anyone had even been staying here.

Next, she reached a bathroom. Again, it looked clean and untouched. As did the first two bedrooms.

At the third bedroom, she paused. If she didn't find anything here, then all this would be for nothing.

Cassidy nudged the door open. She sucked in a breath at what she saw.

A chair had fallen over on the floor beneath a ceiling fan. Beside the chair was a noose and a steak knife. Judging by the battered strands at the end of the noose, someone had cut through the rope.

This was their crime scene, Cassidy realized. The place where Al Hartman's life had ended.

"Bingo," Mac said behind her.

Bingo was right.

Cassidy squinted as something in the carpet caught her eye. Carefully, she walked across the room to get a better look at the mystery object. Squatting, she pulled tweezers from her pocket to pick up a small, colorful chip on the floor.

Actually, it wasn't a chip. It was a coral-colored

press-on nail. Just like the ones Trisha Hartman had been wearing. And the woman had been missing one.

She needed to talk to Trisha again. Now.

And Cassidy knew just where to find her.

CHAPTER TWENTY-TWO

Cassidy had dropped Mac back off at the station so she could talk to Trisha Hartman alone. This was a conversation she wanted to have one-on-one.

Trisha was staying at the only inn in town, and the woman at the front desk had told Cassidy that Trisha was here. Cassidy rapped at the door and waited, anxious to get to the bottom of this.

When Trisha pulled the door open, her eyes looked red, like she'd been crying.

"Chief …" she started, wiping her hands beneath her eyes and trying to compose herself. "What a surprise."

"I have more questions for you," Cassidy's voice sounded hard and her compassion had all but disappeared.

Fear stretched across Trisha's face, through her round eyes and quivering chin. "Do you?"

Did she know she'd been caught?

"I know there's more you're not telling me, Trisha. And every time you hide something, you look guiltier and guiltier."

"I wouldn't have done anything to Al. You've got to believe me." Her face twisted as she stared at Cassidy, pleading with her eyes.

"I'm having a hard time believing anything you've said."

"Okay, okay. I'll tell you the whole story." She raised her hands in defeat.

Cassidy noticed that the woman had finally taken her fake nails off. "I'm waiting."

Trisha opened the door farther. "There are two seats in here. Do you want to come in?"

Cassidy stepped inside, observed the neat room, and then took a seat in a blue armchair near the window. "Go ahead."

Trisha rubbed her hands against her jeans and sat in the chair across from her. "Al called me about a week ago."

"What about?"

"He said he wanted out."

"Wanted out of what? Anthony Gilead's inner circle?" Cassidy clarified.

She nodded quickly, adamantly. "Yes. But he'd given up his car and his cell phone and he had no way to leave. He wanted me to come get him."

That was an interesting development. "What did you say?"

"Al promised to make changes. He said he was a

different person, and he begged me to take him back. Said he missed me and the kids, and he admitted that he'd messed up."

"So you came all the way here?" It was probably an eight-hour drive, not including ferry times.

Trisha focused on the floor. "That's right. I came. I didn't know what else to do but to help. He sounded desperate ... and sincere."

"Did he say what had changed?"

"Not really. He said he'd update me when I got here. So I came and pulled up to the address he'd given me. I walked inside and found him ..." A sob wracked her voice. "I found Al hanging from a ceiling fan. It was so terrible."

Some of Cassidy's irritation with the woman subsided. This woman might not have told the complete truth, but her grief was real. "What did you do?"

"I didn't know what to do, so I cut him down."

"Did you ever think about calling the police, Trisha?"

She dabbed her eyes again with a crumpled tissue. "I knew how it would look. Our divorce proceedings were not pretty. And then I show up right when he's found dead?"

"So you cut him down and left him?"

Trisha shrugged, looking deflated. "I know how that sounds. It sounds bad. I sound guilty. But I wasn't strong enough to take Al anywhere. And I figured the real estate company would find him soon enough.

That no one would even have to know that I'd been there."

"Yet you called me a few days later. What changed?"

"His body washed up in the ocean. When I heard that, I knew he hadn't hung himself. Someone had done it, and they were trying to cover their tracks. They probably thought the ocean would drag him out to sea. But it didn't. It spit him back out." Her tear-filled eyes met Cassidy's. "I'm all my kids have left. Are you going to arrest me?"

Cassidy licked her lips and contemplated her next move. "Not yet. But is there anything else you're not telling me?"

She sniffled, her shoulders sagging with defeat. "There is one other thing."

"Go ahead." Cassidy felt weariness pressing in on her.

She walked over to her nightstand and plucked up a book. "I took this from Al's rental house."

She handed Cassidy a paperback entitled *Finding God's Way in Your Life: 10 Rules to Live By*. The nonfiction title was probably two hundred fifty pages thick with a gentle blue cover, complete with a dove flying into a bright beam of light.

"What is this?"

"It was written by that Anthony Gilead guy. I thought maybe if I read it, it would help me understand why Al had done some of the things he did. Instead, it left me even more confused. I just ... I didn't understand most of what I read. It was unlike any Christian book I've read before."

"I'm going to need to keep this." Cassidy held up the book.

"Please do. I want it gone. I don't want anything else to do with this situation."

"You're not cleared yet, Ms. Hartman. I still need you to stick around on the island. Do you understand?"

Trisha nodded. "I understand. But my children … they miss me. My mom is watching them for me, but I told her I'd be home by tomorrow."

"I'm doing my best to find answers." Cassidy stood and stepped toward the door. "The more forthcoming people are with me, the faster I'll get this figured out."

"I don't know anything else. I promise."

"I'll be in touch soon."

———

TY CAME with Cassidy to monitor the woods on the north end of the Gilead's Cove compound. They'd both changed into dark jeans, dark tops, dark jackets, and dark baseball caps as well as boots. Even in the winter, ticks and other critters had the amazing ability to stay alive out here. Besides, it was bitterly cold—and becoming more so as the sun set.

They tromped through the underbrush until they found a good spot just out of sight of the fence.

"You really think that woman is going to come over

here again?" Ty said, perching on a low-lying branch of a live oak tree.

"I have no idea, but it's worth a shot. Besides, I can see into the compound a little more this way. Maybe I'll discover something."

She sat beside him and filled him in on her day.

"That's crazy," Ty said. "Did you talk to Serena yet and get her take on this Dietrich situation?"

"No, not yet. I actually tried to call her, but she didn't answer. Skye said she drove over to Hatteras to pick up some more supplies for her business, whatever that means. Her ice cream delivery comes by boat every week—or less in the winter. At least that should mean she's far away from Dietrich right now. In the meantime, I asked Skye to keep an eye on her and explain the situation."

Ty picked up a twig and absently twirled it between his fingers. "What do you think of the new guy? Dane? Good choice?"

"He seems competent, and what more can I ask for? I strongly suspect that Leggott will be leaving soon too, so I know I don't have much time to waste. Summer will be here before we know it."

"At least it's a start, right?"

"Right." Cassidy reached into the pocket of her coat and pulled out the book that Trisha had given her. "Let's find out a little more about this movement going on here at Gilead's Cove."

"Anthony Gilead has a book, huh?" Ty glanced at the cover and frowned.

"Apparently. But it's not available anywhere online —I checked. So this must be something that's handed out to members or potential members."

"I'm surprised it's not online so he can spread his message to the hungry masses."

"Maybe he doesn't want to expose his teachings to anyone and everyone—only a select few. There's probably less scrutiny that way. Or maybe this is more of a soft launch, and he's getting some initial feedback."

"I doubt that. He seems too arrogant to think he can fail." Ty tossed the twig he'd been twirling into the brush.

Cassidy squinted as she opened the book midway. She couldn't risk turning a light on for illumination, but the sun was quickly fading. She held the book closer and read the words there. "Listen to this, Ty. He's quoting from what he claims is a noncanonized book of the Bible called Makir."

"Never heard of it."

"Me neither, not that I'm an expert on these things. He claims that God showed him and his team where to find an ancient manuscript for this forgotten book. They had to risk everything while in the Middle East in order to obtain it."

"Including smuggling it out of the country?"

"He doesn't say that. But he does say," Cassidy read the words aloud, "that the old scrolls were exactly where God had promised. Translators had worked around the clock to both preserve the fragile parchment and to translate the words there."

Ty looked at something on his phone, squinting as his eyes scanned his screen. "According to a quick search, it looks like there was someone named Makir in Genesis. He was the father of … Gilead."

"So now it makes a little more sense why Anthony Gilead took on this new name. What it doesn't tell us is who he really is." She swatted a branch that scratched her neck, propelled toward her by the breeze.

"But it does confirm the fact that this man was in the Middle East."

Cassidy studied his face a moment, realizing again just how much this was bothering Ty. "You still think you had contact with him before coming here to Lantern Beach?"

"Maybe not with him directly. But I can't shake the feeling that we're in some way connected." He nodded toward the book again. "What else does it say?"

"There are a lot of quotes from this supposed book of the Bible that talk about being set apart. About giving up everything. About …" Cassidy squirmed and read the passage again, making sure she understood it correctly.

"About what?" Ty leaned closer.

"About those who aren't a part of the movement being an abomination worthy of death." A chill washed over her.

"That sounds ominous … maybe even threatening."

"Yes, it does." Cassidy's mind dwelled on those words. Certainly these followers didn't put that line into practice, did they?

She thought again about that bone Carter Denver's dog had found. They hadn't received the results back yet, but what if it was human? Could it be tied in with all this craziness?

"I'm liking this less and less all the time," Ty said.

So was she.

As something moved in the distance, Cassidy grabbed Ty's arm. "I see someone coming."

They both froze as they watched a woman walk toward the fence.

Cassidy squinted. She'd seen her before.

She was the honey blonde who'd been cleaning the bathrooms.

She was Moriah Roberts.

CHAPTER TWENTY-THREE

Cassidy watched as the woman approached the fence and stared out at the woods, a far-off look in her eyes.

"Let me handle this," Cassidy whispered. She feared a male might scare the woman off. Cassidy might scare her off also, for that matter, but she figured the odds were in her favor.

"You've got this."

Cassidy appreciated Ty's words of encouragement, even more so as jitters rattled through her.

She swallowed hard before stepping forward and calling, "Moriah."

The woman froze. Her gaze stretched through the woods before finally focusing on Cassidy. She startled and took a step back, as if she might run.

"No, wait. Please. I'm not going to hurt you."

Moriah glanced around and then inched closer. "Who are you?"

Cassidy was careful to stay in the shadows, just in case anyone else came past. "I need your help."

Moriah shook her head. "I'm not sure what I can do to help anyone."

"I think a man who was a part of the group you're associated with is dead."

Her eyes widened. "This is a safe place. No one would get hurt here."

"He might have harmed himself. But I need to know for sure if that's the case. I need certainty that no one else harmed him."

"I'm not sure what you want me to do. I was just here to look for deer. They come out at dawn and dusk sometimes, and I like to catch a glimpse of them. If I get caught … they might throw me out."

"I won't tell anyone."

Moriah seemed to contemplate it a moment before backing up. "I'm sorry. I can't help. I can't let anything mess up this opportunity."

Cassidy licked her lips, knowing she needed to proceed carefully. "Your parents are here on the island, Moriah."

She froze again. "What?"

"They came here looking for you. They're worried."

"Tell them I'm okay. Please? My dad has heart problems. I don't want anything to happen to him."

Cassidy didn't want to play this next card, but she felt like she had no other choice. She had to somehow convince Moriah to help her. "Moriah, I can do that. But I need you to do me a favor first."

"Like what?" Moriah's big, doe-like eyes fastened on Cassidy's.

At that moment, Cassidy sensed just how young the girl was. She sensed Moriah's confusion. Her vulnerability.

And she could see where Gilead might seem like the perfect solution.

In Cassidy's mind, that made all of this even more of a crime.

"I need to find out if a guy named Al Hartman was affiliated with Gilead's Cove," Cassidy said.

Moriah blinked and clutched her tunic closer around her neck. "How am I supposed to find that out?"

"Can't you ask around?"

"People will get suspicious if I pull that name out of thin air." She shivered.

Were these people not allowed to have coats? It was bitterly cold outside …

"Moriah, a man that we believe was associated with this group was strangled and then tossed out into the ocean. We also believe that someone behind this fence may know something. Can you keep your ears open for us?" She had to convince Moriah to help her.

She stared at Cassidy a moment as if contemplating her answer.

She didn't respond.

And then she craned her neck, as if she heard someone coming.

"Moriah, I'll be here tomorrow—at dawn and dusk. Please, come back. Same time. Same place." Cassidy slipped into the shadows and waited. A few minutes later, a man approached Moriah and took her elbow, muttering that he'd been looking for her.

Another chill went down Cassidy's spine.

It was the man she'd seen on the dune—the one who'd been watching when Al's body washed ashore. He was a part of Gilead's Cove.

Her chill deepened as she watched the two walk away.

Cassidy had no idea if her plan had worked.

But maybe—just maybe—she'd planted a seed.

———

THE BAD FEELING in Ty's gut continued to grow as he hovered behind a tree, watching Cassidy from a distance. Whatever was going on behind that fence seemed twisted and wrong. And the idea that Cassidy might entangle herself in it made his blood burn.

He'd known the risks when Cassidy took this job. The woman loved justice and wanted to see the innocent prevail and the wicked pay for their offenses. But doing so put her in the line of fire.

He could hardly stomach the thought of it.

He had to find out this Gilead guy's real name.

As soon as Moriah was out of sight, Cassidy made her way back toward him. Ty stepped from behind the tree and followed her as she motioned toward her SUV. Neither dared to speak as they tromped through the woods. Instead, they waited until they were inside her vehicle.

"Do you think that worked?" Ty asked.

Cassidy shook her head. "I wish I could say. But I have no idea. It was worth a shot."

"That woman … she didn't strike me as the type to betray people she has up on a pedestal."

"Me either. But maybe if it means getting a message to her parents, she'll see it differently. As a one-time thing. I don't know. But I'm at a loss here as to how to find out more information."

"I agree that it was worth a try."

Cassidy cranked the engine and started down the road.

As warmth spread through the vehicle, Ty relished the heat. Even with his jacket on, it had been cold out in those woods. He couldn't imagine how cold Moriah must have been wearing only a tunic. He wasn't sure what the rationale might be for not dressing for the weather.

Then again, he wasn't sure what the rationale might be for joining a cult either.

However, in his three decades on this earth, he'd seen a lot. Ty had seen seemingly normal people join terrorist organizations. He'd seen the boy next door transform from a baseball-loving honor student to a suicide bomber.

People's ideals, when mixed with their emotions and feelings of helplessness, could lead to devastation.

"Where do you want to go?" Cassidy asked, pulling

him from his thoughts. "I know you have stuff to do, and I'm probably just going back to the office for now."

As much as Ty would like to stick with Cassidy for the rest of the evening, he knew that wouldn't cut it. The last thing he wanted was to be overbearing or to get in the way of Cassidy's job. He would let her have her space, but he'd also remain on guard.

"If you could drop me back at the cottage, that would be great," he finally said. "I have some paperwork that I need to fill out."

"No problem."

When Cassidy parked in their driveway, Ty pulled Cassidy close until their lips met.

"What was that for?" Cassidy asked, her voice soft as she stared up at him.

Ty brushed a stray hair from her face. "Because I love you."

She smiled. "I love you too."

"I need for you to be careful." His throat burned as he said the words.

"I always am."

"I know, but …" He pressed his lips together, not wanting to sound like a broken record.

Cassidy squeezed his hand. "This whole thing has really shaken you, hasn't it?"

He nodded, unable to deny it. He wasn't someone who was easily shaken, but when the woman he loved was in danger, that was a different story. "Yeah, it has."

"I'll be careful. I promise." She leaned forward and

pressed her lips against his in another kiss. "I'll be home later, okay?"

"I look forward to it." Begrudgingly, he told her goodbye and went inside.

As soon as he got to his computer, he sent a photo of Anthony Gilead to some of his military contacts. Maybe someone would recognize him. Because he couldn't drop this.

No, he *wouldn't* drop this.

There was too much on the line.

CHAPTER TWENTY-FOUR

Moriah couldn't stop thinking about the woman she'd seen in the woods yesterday.

She knew she shouldn't have gone over there. But something about those woods reminded her of her West Virginia home. She used to wander to the edge of her property in the early morning and watch the deer in the fields. She'd listen to the squirrels rustling and even seen the occasional fox or bear.

She'd always loved animals, and each of those glimpses was a treasured memory for her.

It wasn't that she didn't like the water. She did. There was something so serene about it.

But she was more of a mountain type of girl.

"Moriah?" someone said.

She snapped her attention back to the present. She waited in line to be served her breakfast. She moved forward and a glob of oatmeal plopped off a scooper and onto her plate, followed by a syrupy scoop of canned peaches. Her stomach growled. She'd always liked protein in the morning. It helped to keep her blood sugar level balanced.

But she would make sacrifices for the cause.

And she still had that bread in her trailer. She'd had to nibble on it more than once. Having it was a godsend.

Whatever she did, she wouldn't betray Gilead. She wouldn't ask about Al Hartman. She wouldn't believe that anyone here could have hurt him.

No, she'd meant it when she said this was a place of peace. She'd sensed that ever since she arrived.

But her parents ... she hated to think that they were worried about her. What if her dad had a heart attack from his anxiety?

The tray clamored in her hands as her arms began to shake.

"Moriah, we need a word with you," Dietrich said.

Moriah had gathered that Dietrich was one of Gilead's right-hand men. But it was curious. She'd seen him get into a boat and leave the compound in the evenings. Was he not staying here? And, if not, why?

The only other person she'd ever seen leaving the compound was Barnabas. She'd overheard someone saying that he left every Saturday and Wednesday to get gas at the station down the road. Though their goal here was to go off-grid, until that happened they still needed gas for their propane tanks. For heaters.

"Yes, sir," Moriah said.

"Go upstairs and wait outside the door. Gilead will let you in when he's ready."

"Yes, sir." She abandoned her breakfast tray, and her stomach groaned. Though she hadn't been looking forward to eating it, she'd needed something to satisfy her hunger.

But she'd sacrifice for the cause.

A rush of nerves swept over her as she climbed up the dark, wooden steps. The sounds from the cafeteria below became more muted.

Voices drifted from the other side of the closed door. She tried not to listen. But how could she not?

Yet, she could hardly make out anything being said. All she heard was "secret project" and "select few," "very important," and "no one must find out."

What in the world could Gilead be talking about? Whatever it was, it must be important. She felt certain that when the time was right, he'd share the project with everyone.

The door opened, and she lowered her gaze, reminding herself that it was a sign of respect.

Barnabas and a man named Kaleb walked past her. And then she heard Gilead say her name. Her pulse spiked upon hearing his deep tone, upon hearing his voice.

"Yes, Gilead?"

"Come inside," he instructed. "And shut the door."

She did as she was asked. To her surprise, Gilead didn't take his seat on the other side of the desk. Instead, he stood in front of her.

"Moriah, you can look at me."

Her pulse continued to race. She sucked in a deep breath and lifted her head.

Gilead, with his magnetic gaze, stared at her with a gentle, almost mysterious smile on his face.

"I've been watching you since you arrived," he said.

"Have you?" A sudden flutter of nerves came over her.

Had he seen her steal the bread? Had he seen her speaking with that woman in the woods? Would this be the moment when she was kicked out of the Cove?

"I've been very impressed," he said.

What? Had Moriah heard him correctly? She wanted to release her breath but couldn't.

"I'm … I'm glad to hear that."

He stepped closer—close enough that she could feel the body heat coming from him. That she could smell his earthy aftershave—a scent that reminded her of pine trees and leather.

"God has been speaking to me, Moriah."

She waited for him to continue, her heart stuttering out of control.

"I've been praying that He would send me a help-mate. For years, I've muttered the same prayers, and God always told me to wait. Then, just this week, I felt Him urging my heart in a new direction. Toward you."

Her cheeks heated. "I don't know what to say. I'm … I'm honored."

He stooped down closer. "Moriah, I believe that God

has destined us to be together. As one. Overseeing this ministry."

Her? No one had ever said that about Moriah before. She'd always been the laughingstock. The one society discarded. No one had ever seen potential in her before Gilead.

An overwhelming sweep of emotions came over her.

Gilead reached for her, his hands gently caressing her cheek. His touch sent off a million fireworks in her head, and even her skin seemed to come alive.

"I want you to be mine." He gently touched her face with his thumb, rubbing her cheek with tenderness. "But we can't rush this. We can't tell others. Nothing can happen until you go through the initiation process."

"The initiation … when is that?" Moriah asked.

"Now, now. We can't rush it. And no one can know what happens until they are there themselves. It's part of the process." He pulled his hand away, and she instantly missed his touch—craved it.

"So, you don't know how long?" Moriah had always liked timelines. And plans.

"I don't. It will happen when you're ready. Until then, I'd like to continue getting to know you here in my office. What do you think of that idea?"

She could hardly find her voice. "I'd … I'd like that. Very much."

A warm grin spread across his face, and Moriah's pulse surged with delight.

Gilead. Would be hers. She would be his. Together.

Gilead would be everything that Vince wasn't. Together, they could have a happy life.

All of this seemed like a dream come true.

Gilead leaned forward and planted a soft kiss on her forehead.

"I'm so glad we're on the same page," he murmured. "I think our union will be a good thing. God has plans for us, Moriah."

She tried to hold back her giddy smile. "Yes, He does."

As she walked away, resolution formed in her mind.

Nothing could ruin this opportunity for her.

Especially not that lady in the woods.

She'd meet her again today and tell her to pester Barnabas. Barnabas who went to get gas in town. The revelation would get the woman away from Moriah. It would mean a message would be given to her parents.

And Moriah could live out her happy-ever-after here.

CHAPTER TWENTY-FIVE

Cassidy glanced at her watch. It was almost seven now, the sun had already come up, and Moriah still hadn't appeared.

She wasn't coming, was she?

Cassidy had known it was a long shot, but she'd hoped for the best. She certainly needed some kind of good news.

"If you don't find answers this way, you'll find it another way." Ty squeezed her knee.

"I'm going to give it a little more time, just in case."

Cassidy waited until eight thirty and then she stood, figuring the window for Moriah to appear had passed.

Right then, movement in the distance caught her eye.

She sucked in a breath. Could that be Moriah?

Cautiously, Cassidy crept through the woods and peered out from behind a tree. Her pulse spiked.

It *was* Moriah. And she peered through the fence as if looking for something—for Cassidy.

Cassidy stepped out. "You came."

"Only this once." Moriah had a new tone to her voice this morning. Some of her insecurity had slipped away, and something sounding close to defiance replaced it. Was this a trap? Why the change?

"Did you hear anything about Al?"

She shook her head. "No, I didn't. No one will talk to me. But I have other information. If I share it, will you get a message to my parents? And will you leave me alone? I don't want trouble. I have a good life here."

Cassidy bit down a moment. What she really wanted was to get the poor girl out of this situation. But that involved more than this short conversation could contain.

"If that's what you want, Moriah, then I'll leave you alone." *For now.*

"Yes, it's what I want. I can't mess things up. Please, don't ask me to do that."

"What information do you have for me?"

Moriah looked back and forth before leaning closer. "You need to talk to Barnabas."

"Barnabas, the man who handles the front gate?"

Moriah nodded. "He's the one. He knows what goes on here. Not me."

"He's not going to talk to me, Moriah. I've already tried."

Her gaze skittered for a moment. "He goes into town every Wednesday and Saturday to buy gas and a few supplies. You can catch him then, and he might be more willing to talk."

Cassidy let that information wash over her. "Good to know. When does he come into town?"

"He's going tonight. Usually around seven, after it's dark. That's all I can tell you. He's your best bet."

Cassidy nodded. "Thank you, Moriah."

"Now you need to tell my parents I'm okay. I'm happier than I've ever been. I met someone new and wonderful who loves me. And I need you to tell them not to worry about me and that they should go back home."

Cassidy stared through the fence, trying to read her body language. "They want to see you."

"That's not possible right now."

"They're going to have a hard time understanding."

"They don't need to understand it. They just need to do it. It's important to me. Tell them. Tell them I've found a wonderful new life, but it requires privacy for now."

"Gilead won't let you leave. Is that what you're saying?"

Her eyes widened. "Gilead? Gilead is the most self-less person I know. He knows that the world beyond this fence is evil and hurtful, and he's trying to protect us from it."

Cassidy tried to choose her words wisely. "You don't think he's trying to control you?"

A flash of doubt hit Moriah's eyes before quickly disappearing. "Don't be ridiculous. He only wants what's best for us. Now stop feeding me these lies. I've said enough."

She turned to walk away.

"Moriah, there's something you need to know. Vince was found dead. Murdered."

The woman froze, her back to Cassidy. Slowly, she turned around, her lips parted with grief. "What?"

"It's true. I talked to the detective in West Virginia."

At once, Moriah's sorrow disappeared and the defiant look reappeared. "He's not a part of my life anymore. I hate to hear that anyone suffered, but he made my life miserable."

"What if someone associated with Gilead killed him?"

Her eyes widened again. "Why would someone in Gilead kill him? We're not the mafia. We're peaceful and promote love."

"To protect you."

She shook her head in disbelief. "You're talking crazy. You're trying to fill my mind with lies. Just like Vince did. He's probably not even dead, is he? You're just trying to shake me up. I'm done talking to you. Don't come back or I'll call security. Do you understand?"

And, just like that, Moriah was gone.

———

CASSIDY SAT AT HER DESK, biding her time until this evening when they could hopefully corner Barnabas—if

Moriah was telling the truth. Cassidy's gut told her she was, but Cassidy still had to be careful here.

She knew that Barnabas might not talk, so they were going to need a good reason for bringing him into the station.

Cassidy had a mental list. Expired license plates. Out-of-date inspection stickers. Headlights that didn't work properly. Speeding. Credit card issues.

She'd spent the better part of the last hour sending in Ranger's certification and training papers in order to have him added to the department's insurance. If Cassidy was going to do this, she wanted to do it the right way. The boxer would be the department's first police dog. And, tonight, they might need him.

Someone knocked at her office door.

"I bring cake," Lisa said, raising something in her hands.

"I always have time for cake—and friends. And especially friends who are bearing cake."

Lisa grinned and set the plate in front of Cassidy. "I thought you might need a little pick-me-up. I can tell this investigation has you busy and distracted."

"You can say that again." Cassidy paused and stared at the "cake" again. The object on the plate certainly didn't look like any cake Cassidy had seen before.

"You're wondering what kind of cake this is?" Lisa's voice lifted with creative satisfaction and a touch of amusement.

"Or if you're playing a terrible trick on me, and this is actually a moon jellyfish disguised as a cake." The blob in front of her was round and clear with smooth edges. If it wasn't a moon jelly, it could pass for a breast implant.

Lisa laughed. "You're so funny. Of course, I wouldn't do that to you. But it does kind of look like a moon jelly, doesn't it? I'm thinking about playing up that feature this summer. Maybe using a grapefruit slice on the bottom to look like the underside of a jelly fish."

Cassidy wasn't sure how appetizing some people would find that. Then again, there would be some people who might try it just out of fascination and for bragging rights. "So, pray tell. What is this?"

"It's actually a Japanese raindrop cake. In Japanese it's called *mizu shingen mochi*. Anyway, it's a jelly-like dessert made from mineral water and agar powder. You have to be careful and make sure it coagulates correctly in order to get the proper shape."

"Coagulates, huh? Sounds appetizing."

Lisa swiped a hair behind her ear, seemingly unaffected by Cassidy's skepticism. "Isn't it fun? Try it. I mean, if you don't, it will disintegrate after a while. I've still got to work through some of the logistics like that."

Cassidy raised her fork, hesitated only a moment, and then dipped her utensil into the wobbly, oversized raindrop dessert. The first bite melted in her mouth, the most satisfying gelatin dessert she'd ever tried. "This is really good, Lisa."

She beamed. "Thank you. I think it would be a really fun addition to my menu."

Cassidy took another bite. "I agree. People will love this."

"By the way, Clemson came and got the body out of my freezer. I guess the one at the morgue is officially repaired now."

"Good news. Did anyone find out about your secret?"

"Surprisingly, I don't think they did. But every time I hear someone whisper, I get a little paranoid."

"And what are people really whispering about?"

"Probably the dead body."

"Not surprising." Cassidy nodded slowly, then finished the rest of her raindrop cake.

Lisa crossed her legs in the chair, looking like a teenager as she sat there chatting away. "How's the investigation going? I know you can't share details, but are things moving along?"

Cassidy briefly reflected on the highlights of the past couple days. "We're making progress."

"Progress is good. I heard you talked to Rebecca Jarvis."

In a small town, news like that wasn't surprising. "We did. She argued with our victim, but at this point, we have no reason to believe she's guilty."

"I did hear that she's desperate for money." Lisa shrugged. "Not that it would have anything to do with this. But … desperation does funny things. And I heard Carter's dog found a bone?"

"It was sent to the lab for investigation. If it is a human bone, it's most likely from an old grave that the dog dug up. We're not concerned at this point." Even as she said the words, she remembered the text from Gilead's book—about those who didn't believe being an abomination worthy of death.

That bone surely wasn't connected to Anthony Gilead and his followers.

Yet part of her feared it was.

"Danger can't seem to stay away from this island, can it?"

Her words pressed on Cassidy's chest. "No, it can't. No, it most definitely can't."

CHAPTER TWENTY-SIX

"Is everyone in place?" Cassidy asked into the wired communication device attached to her shirt.

She'd borrowed a car from Braden and parked it to the side of the gas station near the air tank. She'd dressed casually and pulled on a baseball cap. Her badge was handy in case she needed it, though.

"Everything's good here."

"We're clear."

"Ready for action."

Dane waited with Ranger in a house right across the street. Leggott was positioned across from the entrance to the compound—in an old field full of discarded boats. He would alert them when Barnabas left to get gas. Mac was inside the station, browsing beef jerky. He'd been giving a rundown on his favorite flavors and which ones made him burp for days afterward. And Ty sat beside her.

Everything was on track. Now she only hoped Barnabas stuck to his normal routine and came out to get that gas.

"Anything yet, Leggott?" Cassidy asked. She stared at the fuel tanks where a lone truck filled up. The cold and darkness would keep a lot of people in tonight.

"No, nothing. No movement at all. If I didn't know better, I'd say there was no one inside this place. It's kind of weird."

Yeah, weird was a good way to describe Gilead's Cove … and the whole Makir prophecy that she'd read about in that book—the very one that Ty was reading right now as he sat beside her.

"You know what doesn't make sense to me?" Ty asked, still staring at the pages. "Even if this Anthony Gilead guy did find this ancient manuscript, it would have probably taken years to translate. Yet he claims he found it five years ago, had it translated, verified by a select group of experts, and now he's proclaiming it as the gospel."

"And even if translating an old, old manuscript like that wasn't an issue, you have to consider the time it would take to verify something like that. And how did the manuscript survive all these years?"

"He claims the scroll was found in some old earthenware vessel and very well preserved. Like he said, God showed him how to find it, and it nearly cost him his life. Which would have been worth sacrificing for the cause because, not only is he God's gift to leadership, but he's also a martyr." Ty's voice faded with disgust.

"Any kind of expedition like that in the Middle East could cost a person his life. But the whole thing sounds fishy to me. I still have no idea how he got this out of the country."

"He could have smuggled it." Ty showed her a page. "Look at this. Gilead has pictures of himself—in the desert. In a research lab bent over the document. Shaking hands with scholars."

"It still sounds like a con to me." He could have hired actors, for all she knew. Cassidy wouldn't put anything past some people.

"I don't buy it either. But for someone who's looking for answers and who's desperate to turn their life around … this could seem legit. He's done a pretty good job presenting this as the truth."

"The best con artists are very good at what they do. That's what makes them so scary."

Cassidy stared out the window, feeling anxious for everything to begin. She glanced at her watch. It was past seven now. Wasn't that when Barnabas usually came out here?

"Listen," Cassidy started. "I know I've been on edge this week. I'm sorry. Things will return to normal when …"

When what, Cassidy? When this cult leaves the island? How are you going to make them do that?

She couldn't, she realized. Best-case scenario, she could catch Gilead doing something illegal, lock him up, and hope the rest of his groupies went home. But she knew the truth was that, even if she managed to nab Gilead, there could very well be someone else waiting in the wings to take over.

No, Gilead's Cove would most likely be a long-term headache. If they were just a peaceful religious group who'd taken up residence on the island, that would be one thing. But she had a feeling this group wasn't peaceful, and the longer they stayed here, the better the chance the rest of the island would feel the ripples of their actions.

Maybe "ripples" wasn't the right word. The tsunami? That was more like it.

"This will pass," Ty murmured. "It may not pass quickly, but it will pass."

Cassidy smiled and squeezed his hand. "Thank you for that reminder."

Yes, even her nightmare with DH-7 had eventually passed. Or mostly passed, she should say. But when she'd been in the middle of the situation? It had felt like the storm would never pass.

She sat up straight as a car pulled up to a gas tank. A man who looked an awful lot like Barnabas stepped out —only he wasn't wearing a tunic and khakis.

"Leggott, did you see a vehicle leave the compound? A silver sedan?" Cassidy asked.

"No, Chief. No one has left. I've been watching."

Cassidy turned to Ty. "I wonder if there's another entrance or exit that we don't know about."

"There must be because that looks like Barnabas to me."

This wasn't the way Cassidy wanted to kick things

off. But she was going to have to skip checking his speed and headlights. Instead, she'd pull out the big guns from the very beginning.

"Okay, everyone in place," Cassidy said. "Let's get this show started."

———

CASSIDY REMAINED IN THE VEHICLE, waiting to see how things would play out before she made her appearance. She watched as Dane strode from the rental house, Ranger on the leash beside him. Dane wore his newly minted police uniform while Ranger had on a vest, indicating he was an official police dog.

Cassidy could hear everything he said over her com. She could hear Dane sweet-talking Ranger. Hear him praising the canine for walking beside him. Even hear him breathing.

"Excuse me, sir. I'm Officer Dane Bradshaw with the Lantern Beach PD, and we're doing random drug checks here today. I wanted to let you know that, as a matter of routine, my dog will be checking out your vehicle."

"Don't you need permission for this?"

"Permission from the county, yes. We've got it."

"This is an invasion of privacy."

"It's perfectly legal, I assure you. If you don't have anything to hide, then this shouldn't be a problem."

From where Cassidy sat, she saw Barnabas's tight, jerky motions. He definitely looked nervous.

"Look, I don't want any trouble," Barnabas said. "I just need some gas and some propane and then I'll be gone. I don't have anything."

As he said the words, Ranger alerted to something in the man's car by sitting down and waiting.

"I'm going to need you to pop your trunk, sir," Dane said.

Barnabas remained silent a moment and then … he started to flee.

And that was Cassidy's cue to emerge.

She hurried from the car. Her legs burned as she pushed herself across the asphalt after their suspect. Barnabas, with his short legs, was no competition for her. She easily caught up with him.

Cassidy lunged and grabbed his arm. They both tumbled to the ground, and Cassidy pulled out cuffs from her waistband.

"If you're not guilty, why are you running, Barnabas?" she asked, restraining his wrists behind him.

He groaned. "All I was supposed to do was get gas."

Cassidy pulled him to his feet. "Let's go see what's in your trunk. You want to unlock it for us? Otherwise, we have our ways."

He groaned again. "Fine. I'll unlock it."

Cassidy practically dragged him back to his truck. Mac and Ty now stood there, along with Dane and Ranger.

"My keys are in the car," Barnabas mumbled.

Cassidy handed Barnabas off to Mac and grabbed

the keys. She opened the trunk, not certain exactly what she thought she'd find inside.

Four propane tanks stared back, along with a gray wool blanket.

Ranger had alerted them. There had to be more to this.

She pulled out the contents of the truck and felt around the edges of the compartment.

As she did, Ranger began barking behind her.

Using her fingers, she pried the bottom of the trunk up.

Her heart beat in her ears as she scanned the rest of the trunk.

And then she realized she'd hit the jackpot.

Pulling on a glove, she picked up one of the small bags tucked beneath the carpet and raised it for inspection. White powder filled it.

"Flakka," she muttered. She'd recognize the drug anywhere.

"I don't know how that got there." Barnabas's voice climbed in pitch. "I swear."

"You've been found in possession of illegal drugs, Barnabas. I'm afraid we're going to have to take you in."

"Please, they'll never accept me back if they find out I've been in your custody. Let me go. Keep the drugs. I don't want them."

"You should have thought about that before you brought drugs onto this island," Mac said.

"But I didn't. I promise. I didn't put them there. This is a community vehicle. I'm just a driver."

Cassidy had her bargaining chip—and he just might be panicked enough to spill what he knew. "Let's talk about it down at the station."

———

BARNABAS HAD BEEN at the station now for three hours. He hadn't spoken a word and had refused any phone calls. Instead, he sat in his holding cell and appeared to be meditating with closed eyes, crossed legs, and upturned palms.

This wasn't exactly how Cassidy had hoped things would go.

The good news was that they had every right to hold the man. He'd been in possession of illegal drugs, and Cassidy had already begun the process of pressing charges against him. Unfortunately, the magistrate came into town only a couple days a week, and today wasn't that day. The isolation of the island made everything take longer at times.

They'd also been able to search Barnabas's vehicle for any other evidence—including anything that might indicate Al had been in that vehicle at some point. It would verify to them that Al was indeed a part of Gilead, since no one inside the organization wanted to admit it.

But it looked like Cassidy would be in for a long night.

Dane remained at the station with her, and Leggott continued to search Barnabas's vehicle and run his plates. Mac and Ty were in the lounge, passing their time there by experimenting on some of that very beef jerky Mac had been giving them commentary on earlier.

Cassidy slipped into her office, giving Barnabas more space to think. She herself could use a quick breather. At her desk, she rubbed her temples and reviewed what she knew so far.

Al had been found on the shore. He'd died from asphyxiation, most likely from a noose around his neck. He showed signs of being beaten with a whip of some sort.

Gilead claimed he didn't know him.

Al's estranged wife lied about coming into town early. She said she found her husband already dead but ran out of fear.

Rebecca the realtor had argued with Al. He didn't want her to let the real estate deal with Gilead go through and claimed the group didn't need to buy any more property on the island.

Though the two women remained suspects, Cassidy's gut told her that this crime was somehow associated with the cult and not Trisha or Rebecca. But, without getting into the gated community, it would be nearly impossible to gain more information. The names she knew so far from being inside were Gilead, Barnabas, Dietrich, Kaleb, and Moriah.

She also needed to consider that Al could have

killed himself. If that was the case, who had put him in the water and why?

Cassidy had so many questions.

Ty knocked on her door. "Anything yet?"

She shook her head. "Not a word."

"You going to wait him out?" Ty lowered himself into the seat across from her.

"For now. After that we'll try to find out ways to put more pressure on. I did run his name through the system, so I know a little more about him."

"What did you find out?"

"His real name is Gary Largo, and he's from Kentucky—near the West Virginia border. He worked in construction until he was busted for prescription drug fraud. He had an accident on the job two years ago and got hooked on painkillers. He was evicted from his home and living on the streets last year at this time."

"Sounds like just the type of person Gilead might prey on."

"My thoughts exactly. We tested his blood alcohol level, and he's clean."

"Has he been branded?" Ty asked.

Cassidy cringed as she remembered seeing the mark on the man's back. They'd taken a picture of it when he'd been booked. "He has been, but, again, he doesn't want to talk about it. He doesn't appear to have any close family, so I can't use them for leverage."

"What can you use?"

That was a great question, one that she'd been pondering herself. "The only thing I can think of to use is Gilead. Barnabas seems very concerned about being disassociated with them."

"They may be all he has."

"That could be true." Cassidy glanced at her watch and stood. "It's about time for me to try and get some answers out of him again. Hopefully, I'll have better luck this time."

CHAPTER TWENTY-SEVEN

"You going to tell me where those drugs came from?" Cassidy stared at Barnabas. At the sweat sprinkled at his hairline. At the way his hands trembled.

He had refused to talk—until Cassidy had offered him some Mountain Dew and a Snickers candy bar. She'd talked to the attendant at the gas station, who'd told her that Barnabas always purchased those two items when he came in. Apparently, they were his weakness.

Cassidy would guess that junk food wasn't allowed inside the compound.

Either way, it had worked. Barnabas had come out of his meditative pose and seemed human again.

"I'm telling you—I had no idea they were back there. I didn't look beneath the floor covering in the trunk. I'm only using this vehicle to do errands for Gilead."

"Whose vehicle is it?" Cassidy already knew who it

was registered to, but she wanted to hear what Barnabas would say.

"I'm not sure."

She leaned closer, the bright lights of the tiny room unforgiving. "Barnabas, you see everyone who comes and goes from the compound. Certainly you know whose vehicle it is."

As moisture trickled down his temple, he tried to wipe his forehead against his shoulder. "We surrender our vehicles when we pledge to Gilead."

"Obviously, something happens to those vehicles after they're surrendered."

"Gilead keeps a few for emergencies—he doesn't keep them on the property, though."

"And who does this car belong to?"

He swallowed hard. "I think it belongs to Kaleb."

Cassidy straightened, careful not to show any nerves. With each passing moment, she could feel Barnabas's anxiety building. She hoped to use that to her advantage. The small room with two chairs and a table would make anyone feel apprehensive.

"What do you know about Al Hartman?" Cassidy asked.

Barnabas blinked. "Is that what this is about? You just wanted to nab me on some bogus charges so you could question me about another crime?"

"There were drugs found in your vehicle. Those aren't bogus charges."

He said nothing.

"And your response indicates that you did know Al, and you know he was murdered."

"I heard you talking to Gilead about it." The sweat glistened even more.

"Do you know what happened to him, Barnabas?"

"No! I don't even know him."

"We know that he was a part of your movement. His wife found a book by Anthony Gilead in his possession. You can stop denying the facts."

Barnabas closed his eyes and shook his head. "I came here for peace, not trouble."

Cassidy leaned closer and lowered her voice. "Then tell me what you know. We can strike a deal."

"I don't want a deal. I just want to go back. Please... I have no future without Gilead."

"You almost sound scared. Are you afraid if Gilead finds out about this that he'll hurt you like he hurt Al?"

"No! Not at all. You're putting words in my mouth."

Her gaze burned a hole in him. "I'm just trying to find out the truth. And if you really want some peace in your life, why don't you tell me what's going on? Just you and me. Right here. It will get a load off your chest."

"You'll use whatever I say against me."

"I think you'll feel better. You just need to talk to me. I know about the accident you were in. I know about how you got addicted to painkillers. How you lost your house. How you lost everything. Gilead took you in, and I'm sure you owe him a lot."

"I do."

Cassidy leveled her gaze with his. "But you don't owe him your life."

Barnabas's hands hit the table. "Yes, I do!"

"You owe him so much that you'll go to prison for him?" Cassidy asked.

He said nothing.

And Cassidy supposed that was answer enough.

———

WHILE CASSIDY INTERROGATED BARNABAS, Ty remained in her office and called one of his old military contacts again. Buddy Alan had been one of the SEAL team commanders Ty had worked with. The man was still in the Navy, now working in a management position instead of in the field.

"What can I do for you?" Hearing Buddy's deep voice brought back a slew of memories for Ty—times of heroics, times of tragedy and grief, of victory, of defeat. There were so many emotions that accompanied Ty's service in the military.

Ty leaned his shoulder against the wall. "Buddy, it's been a while, but I have a question for you."

"Shoot."

"You remember that mission we went on, the one where we were sent to rescue a government official who was being held captive in Iraq?"

"I don't think any of us will forget him."

Usually, before starting a mission, their team had more information. On occasion, a case was high profile and getting media attention, so many details were even public. But this guy that they'd rescued was like a ghost. The military hadn't given *any* information, and the media remained clueless about the fact that the man was ever captured, even.

The team had been given this man's location and orders to rescue him, but nothing else. Not even a name. Just a photo. The mission had been risky, and one of their guys had taken a bullet. Thankfully, he'd recovered and been able to resume a normal life.

"Yeah, the whole mission was kind of strange, but it wasn't our job to ask questions," Ty continued. "We were sent in to rescue that guy from a terrorist compound, and that's what we did."

"What do you need to know?" Buddy asked.

"When we rescued this guy, he was … a mangled mess. Unrecognizable." Ty still flinched when he remembered how they'd found the man. They'd thought he was dead, but, when they checked, he still had a faint heartbeat.

"He'd been beaten so badly we weren't sure it was him," Buddy said. "I've never seen someone's face so swollen. His back was like raw meat."

Ty swallowed hard. "His rescue never made the news. There weren't any follow-ups or updates. It was almost like it hadn't happened."

"That's correct."

Except for the fact that the event had changed his life and the lives of his comrades. A person didn't see another human in that state of suffering and return to the previous state of normal. No, seeing what they had that day changed every one of them.

Rumor had it that the man had been doing some deep cover work within some terrorist groups. The government probably thought that putting his face and name out there would only bring danger to those he loved. They were probably right.

"I know this is going to sound like a strange question, but do you have any pictures of this man? Maybe a copy of the one we were given before we went in to identify him?"

Buddy paused for a beat. "You want a picture of him?"

"There's a situation that's come up here where I'm living now, and I can't shake the feeling that it may be somehow connected with that rescue. Maybe even to that man."

"Why in the world would something be connected?"

If only Ty knew that answer. "I don't know. That's what I'm trying to figure out."

Another second of silence passed. "I see. I should be able to find the photo. I can send you what I know—off the record. You can't share this with anyone."

"You know I won't. It's for purely personal reasons."

"I'll see what I can find and send it to your email—unofficially, of course. I'm trusting you on this one."

Ty ended the call and waited. Buddy was reliable, and he knew the man would do as he promised. Ty also knew this could lead nowhere. But he had to know.

A few minutes later, his phone buzzed.

It was Buddy. He'd sent the email.

With bated breath, Ty opened the attachment.

A photo stared back at him.

A photo of a man in his late twenties with short brown hair.

And the man looked nothing like Anthony Gilead.

Ty released his breath. It had been worth a try. But he still had no idea if this was truly connected to Ty's former work as a SEAL or if he was reading way too much into this.

CHAPTER TWENTY-EIGHT

"Barnabas, Al Hartman has a wife and children who need answers," Cassidy continued, not ready to give up. "How can you have peace knowing that they're suffering and that you could provide relief to them?"

He squirmed in his seat, his hands cuffed to a bar on the table. "I told you, I don't know what you're talking about."

"I don't know a lot about this movement you're a part of, but I do know you promote truth and love and acceptance. What better way to show love than by ending someone's agony?"

He said nothing, but the sweat continued to bead over his skin.

"I have all night, Barnabas." And she did. Patience was the best way to get someone to talk sometimes.

Barnabas's fingers began to inch back and forth as if trying to work out an internal, unseen pressure.

"Al was one of us," he finally said, his voice quivering. "But he was depressed. None of us were surprised when he took his own life."

Finally, Cassidy was getting somewhere. "So you knew he hung himself?"

Barnabas nodded. "I heard. I guess he'd been threatening to do it for a while. I just didn't think he really would. He was a changed man after joining us. He had so much potential."

"So you don't believe anyone did this to him?"

"No, I don't believe so."

Cassidy shifted and softened her expression, feeling on the verge of discovering the truth. "Barnabas, why was he living in a house off the compound?"

Barnabas opened his mouth. But before any words could leave his lips, the door behind her opened and … Kaleb stepped in.

"He's not going to answer any more questions without me here." Gone was the wounded, branded man Cassidy had met a few nights before. This Kaleb looked professional, tough, and confident.

"Are you a lawyer?" Cassidy sprang to her feet, wondering who had let him in. In the background, she spotted Dane. He shook his head apologetically.

"As a matter of fact, I am," Kaleb said. "And I'll be representing him."

Cassidy's chest tightened. This put a wrench in her plans, to say the least. Barnabas had been on the verge of sharing more.

Kaleb's eagle-eyed gaze simmered on Cassidy's. "And, aside from the fact that I'm telling him to remain silent, I also have evidence that will prove he's innocent of the charges against him."

"How do you know the charges against him?" Cassidy watched his face.

"When he didn't come back to the compound, I came here. Some guys outside the police station were talking about someone being arrested on drug charges. I put the pieces together."

Cassidy found that unlikely, but there had been passersby outside during the man's arrest. Someone could have overheard something. That didn't explain how or why Kaleb had already been dressed in a suit when he arrived here.

"And what's this evidence you have?" she asked.

"He was driving my vehicle so if anyone should be arrested for drug possession, it's me. Barnabas knew nothing about the flakka found there."

Cassidy bristled more. Another twist she hadn't seen coming. "Do you care to explain why you had drugs in your possession?"

Kaleb frowned. "It's because of my brother. I let him use my vehicle several times, and he had a severe drug addiction—to flakka. I thought he got rid of all of his supply. I paid for him to get clean. But he must have hidden some in my trunk without me knowing."

"I'm going to need to talk to your brother to confirm this," Cassidy said.

"I wish you could, but he died of an overdose three months ago. If you check online, you can confirm that."

Leggott knocked on the window behind her.

"Excuse me one minute."

She stepped into the hallway, grateful for the chance to clear her head. "Yes?"

"I just got the results of the drug test," Leggott said. "Barnabas didn't have any in his system. I just thought you'd want to know."

She bit down. She may not have a reason to keep him here.

And that was terribly unfortunate.

———

"YOU HAD TO LET BARNABAS GO?" Ty's voice held disbelief.

Cassidy raked a hand through her hair as she sat at her desk. "I had no choice. I didn't have enough to hold him, especially not when Kaleb confessed that the drugs were actually his. His brother's, to be precise. We still have Kaleb in custody, and we'll question him more —or try to—but he's not saying anything. There's nothing more we can do until the magistrate gets into town."

"Did someone pick Barnabas up?" Ty continued.

"No, he took Kaleb's car. Kaleb's other car, not the one the drugs were found in."

"I'm assuming you searched that car as well?"

"We did. It was clean. And it was registered to Kaleb." She let out a sigh.

"I'm sorry, Cassidy."

"I was so close to getting answers, Ty. Barnabas

admitted that Al was one of them. That he was depressed but that no one thought he was suicidal."

"What if that's all this is, Cassidy? What if he took his own life? There's no crime in that—not legally, at least."

"Even if he took his own life, someone put him in the water. Someone left those scars on his back. He can't speak for himself right now, so I'm determined to speak for him."

"That's admirable."

"What I need is someone on the inside." She tapped her fingernails on her desk.

"I'll do it."

Cassidy turned as a new voice entered the room, and alarm raced through her. "Serena ... what are you doing here?"

"I just got back and heard the news," she said. "I'm the perfect one to go inside, Cassidy. I can convince Dietrich to convert me."

"That's absolutely, positively the worst idea that I've heard in a long time. By no means would I send you into that lion's den." Cassidy's hand sliced through the air.

"I can handle it." Serena stared back. The happy-go-lucky girl had a touch of bitterness in her eyes.

Cassidy supposed it didn't matter how easygoing a person was. Betrayal still hurt and could transform normally placid emotions into untamable beasts.

"I'm not even sure a trained officer of the law could handle it, Serena." The idea was bad on so many levels.

"I make the most sense." She crossed her arms stubbornly.

Cassidy shook her head. "I mean it, Serena. Absolutely not. You're not to go near that compound."

Serena shrugged, almost like she was half-listening, and a spike of fear went through Cassidy. The girl was just brazen enough that she might try, despite what Cassidy told her.

Cassidy swallowed hard, trying to keep her emotions in check. "Why'd you come by, Serena?"

"Because Skye just told me about Dietrich. I wanted to hear it from you."

"It's true, Serena," Cassidy said. "He's one of them. Has he tried to convert you yet?"

She shook her head. "No, he hasn't. I had no idea. He seemed so normal."

"I'm sure that outside the compound many of the members seem normal. And many of them may be harmless, just sheep being led into a slaughterhouse. But that doesn't mean you should be around them."

Serena frowned and said nothing for a moment until her lips finally pulled down in a pouty frown. "Dietrich was really nice too."

"There are plenty of nice guys who aren't in cults," Ty reminded her.

"But do they look like Ryan Reynolds?"

Cassidy closed her eyes and let out a sigh. "Serena, please tell me you'll stay away from him. Promise me."

Her frown deepened, but she said nothing.

"Serena …" Ty said. "You deserve someone of quality. You don't want to be pulled into this mess. You might not make it out alive, and you definitely won't make it out unscathed. Hold out for better than that."

Serena didn't say anything for a moment as she seemed to process Ty's words. She'd always had the man up on a pedestal. Maybe Serena would listen to him.

Finally, Serena nodded, even as her shoulders sagged. "Okay. I promise. I'll stay away—from Dietrich and Gilead's Cove."

Even though Serena said the words, Cassidy didn't quite have the confidence that she would follow through.

And that thought would cause Cassidy to lose sleep.

CHAPTER TWENTY-NINE

Cassidy sent Ty to keep an eye on Serena. Meanwhile, Mac and Leggott were watching the compound. Cassidy stood in their "lab," which, in reality, was just an old storage closet at the station where they could do minimal crime scene tests—mostly fingerprints.

There had to be something she was missing, and she wouldn't rest until she figured out what it was.

She pulled out the boxes of evidence they'd collected when Al Hartman washed ashore and began looking through them. His clothes were bagged. Evidence from beneath his fingernails. A hair sample.

Pausing, she held up the bag containing the hair. The piece had been found wrapped around one of the buttons on his shirt, and they'd kept it in case they needed to compare this sample with a potential killer's.

She raised the bag up to the light and frowned. She hadn't noticed it before—hadn't really thought about finding a match. But now that she looked at the hair more closely …

Out of curiosity, she pulled out another file. This one was the evidence they'd taken on Barnabas, including fingerprints, a mouth swab, and a hair sample. She held both bags to the light to examine them more closely. Both strands had the same red sheen to them. Were the same length.

Her evaluation would never hold up in a court of law. They'd need further testing.

But she felt certain both of these hairs had come from Barnabas.

Which meant that Barnabas had been near Al when he'd died or shortly after.

Her heart skipped a beat.

She needed to get a search warrant to check out Barnabas's quarters.

Maybe this was the missing link they'd been looking for.

———

TWO HOURS LATER, she had her search warrant and headed to the compound. Dane had to drop Ranger off, but he was going to meet her there. She wouldn't go inside without him.

As she headed down the road, she slowed when she spotted a vehicle parked in the driveway of a house right off the main road. Was that …?

It was.

It was the car Kaleb had driven to the station. Cassidy had caught a glimpse of it before Barnabas left. Had Barnabas not gone back to the compound? Was this one of the properties Gilead had bought?

Cassidy pulled up in front of the property. Maybe she'd see if she could catch Barnabas here. However, she would call Dane and have him meet her here instead.

No careless mistakes. *Carelessness leads to failure.*

Another Day-at-a-Glance quote. They always hit Cassidy right when she needed them.

Why would Gilead be buying up properties here on the island?

She had a feeling this would turn into something bigger than the island could handle. She fully expected that, by the end of this, she'd need to call in for help from the state police, the NC State Bureau of Investigation, maybe even the FBI.

Situations like these rarely ended well.

A shadow at the back of the property drew her attention. Was someone there? If so, what were they doing?

Picking up her phone, she called Dane and told him where she was. He was only five minutes away and would meet her here.

Cautiously, she walked around the perimeter of the house to the backyard. She stopped once she had a view of the entire space.

There was no one back here. Just an old shed, a few shrubby trees, and sandy grass.

Strange. Had she been seeing things? It was a possibility.

She turned to go back and wait for Dane.

But she'd only taken a step when something came down hard on her head.

And everything went black.

CHAPTER THIRTY

Cassidy jerked her eyes open and moaned.

Where was she?

She tried to move, but she couldn't. Her arms and legs had been tied to a chair. Everything around her was dark. And the faint scent of smoke filled her lungs.

What …?

Then everything rushed back to her.

Seeing the car Barnabas had taken from the station parked in a driveway. Walking toward the backyard. And then feeling a horrible pain at the back of her head.

Someone had knocked her out and brought her … here.

But where was here?

She glanced around, her eyes adjusting to the darkness.

She appeared to be in an old house with dark wood paneling.

As she took another breath, the scent of smoke became stronger. Was something … on fire?

At a sound behind her, she craned her neck and gasped. Barnabas knelt in front of an old fireplace nursing a fire.

She struggled against the ropes holding her down, but it was no use. She was tied up tight.

"I see you're awake now." Barnabas stepped from the shadows.

Barnabas …

Cassidy coughed. "Why are you doing this, Barnabas?"

"Because I know you're going to keep pushing and pushing, and you'll ruin everything. I can't let you do that. I vowed to be a protector."

"A protector of what?"

"A protector of The Way."

She struggled again, desperate to get away. "Barnabas, there are other means to protect The Way. You don't need to hold me captive."

"Maybe. But I think Gilead will be pleased with this. Maybe he'll even accept me back to the compound."

"Gilead put you up to this?"

A strange smile crossed his face. He was high, she realized. Had he taken some flakka?

"No, of course not. He would never do that. But he says those who don't believe are an abomination. You're not a believer."

So people did take that verse from the book of Makir seriously.

"Did you park in that driveway just to get my attention?" Cassidy asked.

"I figured you'd head to the compound. I also knew you'd pass that house and my vehicle. I knew it was the only way to get your attention. And it worked. Forgive me, but I had to remedy this situation. I couldn't let you ruin everything."

"Barnabas, you really need to think this through." The flames behind her grew. She could hear them. Feel them.

He put the end of a stick in the fire and watched it light. He gently drew it out and said, "Oh, I've been thinking. A lot. And this is the only way."

"Is that what you said when you killed Al?" She struggled, trying to jerk her hands free, even if it required pulling off half her skin.

"He wanted to spread lies about us. He wanted to leave. He could have ruined everything."

"So you hung him with a noose and tried to make it look like suicide? Then you put him in the ocean, hoping he'd wash out to sea, never to be seen again?" There were holes in his story. Like why hadn't he taken the noose? Why had he left it?

"I didn't kill him. I just reminded him what a wretched person he was. How much he'd messed up. How even his own family no longer liked him." He held the burning stick near old, dusty curtains. Not quite touching them, just watching the flames flickering closely.

"And he took his own life." Cassidy's stomach

squeezed with disgust. He'd coerced this man into committing suicide.

Hoping to distract him, she blurted, "Why did you put him in the ocean?"

"He told me once that he'd always wanted to be buried at sea. So I thought I'd help him." The curtains burst into flame in a macabre dance.

"What about the scars on his back?" The fire felt so hot that Cassidy nearly thought her hair was on fire. But it wasn't. Not yet.

She knew an old house like this would burn quickly, but she wasn't sure how much longer she had.

Certainly by now someone had seen the flames in the window. They would call the fire department, and help would be on the way.

Almost as if Barnabas could read her mind, he smiled again. "We're pretty secluded out here. It's going to take a while for anyone to notice this."

Cassidy lifted a prayer, unsure how exactly she was going to get out of this situation alive.

———

TY DIDN'T RECOGNIZE the number on his cell phone, but he answered anyway. If someone was calling him at three in the morning, it had to be important.

"Ty? This is Dane. Is the chief with you?"

Ty's back went straight. "No, she said she was with you."

"We'd planned on meeting at Gilead's Cove, but she

called and said she saw Barnabas's car at a house she passed by. She told me she'd wait for me there. But when I pulled up, her SUV had been parked in the driveway, but the chief was nowhere to be found."

Worry surged through Ty. Something was wrong. Majorly wrong. "Did you check the surrounding houses?"

"I did. I didn't see her."

"I'm going to call Mac, get him to help. We've got to find her, Dane."

"What can I do?"

"Call Rebecca Jarvis. I need to know about any other properties the gang at Gilead's Cove own. She should have those addresses. You're going to have to wake her up, but tell her it's official police business."

"Will do."

Ty lowered the phone and lifted a prayer. This wasn't good. If someone from Gilead's Cove got their hands on Cassidy … he didn't want to think about what could happen. He couldn't let his thoughts go there now.

Wasting no more time, he called Mac and then Wes, who promised to let the rest of the gang know what was going on.

The list of houses Dane would get from Rebecca was their best option. Otherwise, Ty would head to the Gilead's Cove compound himself—and he'd make no apologies about it.

Ten minutes later, Dane called back. He had the list of four houses, and they decided that Ty, Dane, Mac, and Leggott would divide and conquer. They'd split into pairs and take two houses each.

They searched each of those properties but found nothing. No Cassidy.

Ty's worry grew.

Ty and Dane went back to the driveway of the house where Cassidy's SUV had been left to regroup. Ty was trying to gather his thoughts when his phone rang again. It was Rebecca.

"This could be nothing, but there's one other property these guys have looked at," Rebecca said. "I would have told you about it earlier, but I didn't know. My husband actually heard about the deal through some of his fishing buddies. Anyway, the transaction hasn't closed yet, but they did put a contract on this property."

"What's the address?"

Ty put his truck into Drive and took off down the road. The address wasn't far away. If he remembered correctly, this house sat farther off the main road and out of sight, thanks to a line of trees.

If they didn't find Cassidy there ... he had no idea where to search next.

As he pulled up, Ty sucked in a breath.

This was the house ... and it was on fire.

CHAPTER THIRTY-ONE

"Barnabas, you've got to let me go or we're both going to die." Sweat poured down Cassidy's face, and her breaths were labored. The fire had moved from the curtains to the wall. The paneling steadily burned and smoke clouded the room.

"I'm ready to die. Are you?" He said the words calmly, evenly, like he'd already thought about it. A lot. Too much.

Another pulse of fear went through her, and she coughed violently. "Am I ready? Yes. Do I want to? No. Why do you want to, Barnabas?"

"I'm probably going to go to jail anyway."

She shook her head, desperate to get through to him. "Not necessarily. You didn't kill Al. You only moved his body."

"The law isn't on my side. You want to bring us down. Gilead told us."

Her fear turned into anger. "Gilead doesn't always tell the truth."

Barnabas raised his chin in disagreement. "Gilead is the best thing to happen to me."

"Al didn't think so."

"Al became disillusioned. He thought we were giving Gilead too much power." He hacked as the air in the room grew hazy, and he sank to his knees, away from the smoke.

Now she was getting somewhere. She leaned forward to escape the worst of the smoke that pooled on the ceiling. She only hoped she didn't die before she could share what she'd finally learned. "What caused the change?"

"He wanted to leave. To go back to his wife and kids. Gilead told him he couldn't. That he'd pledged his loyalty to The Cause."

It sounded downright creepy to Cassidy. She coughed again before asking, "Was Gilead going to kill him?"

"Gilead? No, he wouldn't do something like that."

More sweat poured down her, and the heat was almost unbearable. She glanced up. The fire climbed inexorably to the ceiling. This whole place would come down soon.

"Barnabas, we've got to get out of here."

"I'm not going anywhere."

He'd given up, hadn't he? He was done. He didn't care anymore. How was she going to get through to him? "Barnabas, the house is going to be consumed in a minute. There will be no going back."

"I know."

Another chill went through her, despite the heat. How would she get out of this one? She had no idea. The ropes pulled too tight. The fire licked too close. Help seemed too far away.

Just as the thoughts pummeled her, she heard a crash.

Was that the door?

Barnabas's eyes widened. He'd heard it too.

He stood and, instead of running toward the sound, he darted toward the back of the house. Another door slammed.

Had Barnabas ... had he just locked himself in a back bedroom?

Cassidy's gaze jerked to the side before a coughing fit captured her. She toppled the chair over so she was lying on the floor, where she could breathe easier. She wouldn't be able to fight this much longer. Soon the smoke would claim her.

But as she pulled her eyes back open, a figure came into view.

Ty.

He was here.

Or was she seeing things?

He rushed toward her and worked the ropes behind her, the smoke already causing him to cough. "I've got you, Cassidy. It's going to be okay."

She couldn't respond, only cough. Try to stay alert. Pray that Ty didn't get injured while trying to save her.

A moment later, her hands were free. Ty gathered her in his arms and bolted toward the door.

"Barnabas," she finally croaked.

"What?"

"Barnabas … went … to … the …back."

"Barnabas is still here?"

She nodded.

"I'll go find him," someone else said.

Dane, Cassidy realized. Dane was here also.

In the distance, she thought she heard sirens over the roar of the fire.

Flames were everywhere. On all the walls. The ceiling. Licking at the floor.

"No," Cassidy rasped. "Wait for the fire trucks. You won't come back out alive."

She squeezed her eyes shut, fighting to remain lucid. Ty's strong arms held her, carried her, just like they'd done so many times before.

They didn't have much time.

A beam fell in front of them.

Ty skirted around it and dashed through the doorway.

The next instant, they were outside.

Cassidy gulped in deep breaths of fresh air. She could breathe again. The air was still smoky, but nothing like inside.

Ty didn't stop walking until he was at his truck. He laid her inside on the seat and then peered at her, brushing her hair back from her face. "An ambulance will be here soon."

She nodded toward the house, wishing his words made her feel better. But there was still so much on the line here.

Wait. Where was …

"Dane," she muttered.

Ty glanced back. He must have gone inside anyway.

Neither said anything. Cassidy and Ty both knew the whole place would be destroyed soon. If Dane didn't get out within the next few minutes with Barnabas …

Just then, someone staggered from the front door.

Dane.

But he was alone.

He jerked down a T-shirt he'd tied over his mouth and bent over, coughing. Then he staggered toward them.

"I found Barnabas," he started, more coughs wracking his body. "But when he saw me, he ran into a bathroom. Locked the door. I couldn't get to him. I don't think he wanted me to."

He didn't. But Cassidy couldn't say the words out loud. Not now. Right now, she needed some water.

But, as she looked up, the entire house collapsed with the fire.

It was too late for Barnabas, she realized. And that was exactly what he'd wanted.

CHAPTER THIRTY-TWO

Four hours later, the sun had risen. Cassidy had a blanket around her and coffee in hand. She'd already been given oxygen and breathed easier. She'd promised the medics she'd go to the clinic for her lungs to be checked out, but she wasn't ready to leave the scene yet.

The same couldn't be said for Barnabas. Firefighters had found his body in the bathroom, just as Dane had said they would.

He'd wanted to die today.

"So do you have enough to arrest Anthony Gilead?" Ty asked, leaning next to her against the back of his ash-covered truck.

Cassidy frowned, wishing she had a different answer. "No, I don't. Besides, anything Barnabas told me went with him to the grave. I have nothing to help me move forward in a legal case."

"Do you believe what Barnabas told you? That Al

hung himself, and all Barnabas did was bury his body at sea, just like Al had wanted."

Cassidy couldn't stop thinking about it herself. "I called Trisha while you were talking to the firefighters. Trisha confirmed that Al had said that before, so Barnabas could have been telling the truth. But the man taunted Al, telling him things that drove him to kill himself. He may not have put the noose around his neck, but he was still guilty, as far as I'm concerned."

Ty frowned as he stared at the remains of the house in the distance, and a moment of silence washed between them.

"I'd like to say this is finally over, but I don't know if it is," Ty said.

"I feel the same way." Cassidy pulled the blanket closer and followed Ty's gaze. Two firetrucks were here. Locals had come out to see what the commotion was. Mac had shown up to keep tabs on the town.

She still had Kaleb in custody, but she was doubtful the charges would stick. He would be a great source of information, but the look in his eyes clearly showed intelligence. He wouldn't be as easy as Barnabas had been to pry answers from.

Cassidy also needed to figure out where this other entrance and exit from Gilead's Cove was. Leggott said no one had come or gone from the compound as he watched this evening. That meant there was more to the place than Cassidy had assumed.

Dane stepped up to her just then, embers of tonight's tragedy staining his new police uniform. He was lucky to have gotten out of that house alive. They all were.

"You okay, Chief?" he asked.

She nodded. "I am. You've had an exciting first day."

His lip curled in a half-smile. "Yes, I have."

"Thank you for all you've done so far. We're happy to have you on board here in Lantern Beach."

"Of course. It looks like it's not going to be such a boring place to work, after all."

"No, it's not." Especially not with Gilead's Cove still as a part of this town.

Cassidy's phone rang, and she glanced down at the screen. Her stomach clenched. It was her mom.

"I should probably take this," she said.

But she didn't bother to move away from Ty. Anything she had to say, he could hear.

"The press conference is later this morning," her mom started. "I haven't been able to sleep all night, so I wanted to give you a call first thing. What did you decide?"

Cassidy swallowed hard before saying, "I can't do it, Mom. I'm sorry. But my life is here."

Ty wrapped his arm around her shoulders, and Cassidy leaned into his strength.

"I was afraid you'd say that," her mom said. "I'm … I'm disappointed."

"I'm sorry, Mom. But that isn't the life for me."

"It could be! Please. Reconsider."

But there was no way Cassidy could go back.

Her mom went on to say there would be a press conference in four hours to tell people what had happened to Cassidy's father. They expected stock in the company to drop. The way her mom talked, the company would never recover.

But Apple had remained strong after Steve Jobs died. Alpha Tech would find the right leader. It would just take time. And that leader wasn't Cassidy. She was still struggling to find her footing and manage a small police department.

With her father's company? The world would be watching. Investors would be watching.

It wasn't the life she wanted for herself.

That company … it might be her Gilead. Her pressure point. The thing that pushed her to be and do things she didn't want.

No, Cassidy was her own person and had to make her own choices.

An invisible weight pressed on her as she hung up.

Ty kissed her forehead. "You okay?"

"Yeah, I'll be fine." She stared out over the house still, her soul feeling restless. "I just have to figure out what to do now."

Who was Anthony Gilead really? What exactly was he planning? Was he connected to Ty's past somehow? And what about the bone Carter Denver's dog had found?

The questions still swirled in her head. She may have wrapped up one mystery, but she still wasn't at peace.

"This town needs you, Cassidy," Ty said. "And so do I."

Cassidy didn't want to let anyone down. But . . . "Anthony Gilead . . . Gilead's Cove . . . they're both different than DH-7. Sometimes I feel out of my element. I'm not sure how to protect Lantern Beach from these people. That scares me."

"You just wait for them to mess up."

That was right. Because they would mess up. And when they did, Cassidy would be there to catch them.

COMING IN FEBRUARY: ATTEMPT TO LOCATE

CHAPTER 1

"Moriah, it's time."

Moriah Roberts stood from the stiff bed nestled on the side of her assigned RV and straightened the tunic she wore. A slight tremble raked through her limbs as she tried to comprehend the scope of what was about to happen.

"Thank you, Ruth," Moriah murmured to the woman standing in the doorway.

"There's no need to be nervous." The permanent frown on Ruth's face deepened, and her self-righteous pallor nearly glowed with piousness. "This should be an honor."

Moriah lowered her head as the reprimand echoed in her mind. The woman could chide the wind for being cold, and Moriah was certain the wind would feel guilted into changing directions.

"It is an honor." Moriah kept her voice soft and nonconfrontational. "But I just don't know what to expect. Everyone has been so secretive."

"They're secretive because this is special. If people spoke openly about our ceremony, then it would lessen its importance." Ruth grabbed a towel from a drawer and wiped some mud from the side of the doorway. The woman was always the mother hen.

Even though the two were officially roommates, the arrangement had never felt equal. Ruth was obviously more strong-willed and, therefore, the boss. She'd also been part of Gilead's Cove longer. Ruth was the one with robust opinions, unwavering confidence, and a knack for remembering every rule that needed to be followed.

Moriah took a step toward the door. She still felt nervous, but she wouldn't tell Ruth that—not unless she wanted another lecture. Besides, Ruth would probably report her shortcomings to the Council and then they wouldn't think she was worthy.

The Council wouldn't tell Moriah that. No, but they'd demote her to cleaning the bathrooms again. At least, that was what she feared. She *hated* cleaning bathrooms almost as much as she'd hated her now-deceased ex-husband Vince.

"Come on now. The Council is waiting for you." Ruth extended her hand to hasten Moriah outside.

As soon as Moriah stepped from the RV and into the dark evening, a cold wind hit her. It was April now, but she'd thought the temperatures would warm up here on Lantern Beach. It had, Moriah supposed. For a couple days. But now it was cold again. The warm weather wouldn't be here to stay until the end of May. That's what Gilead had told her.

A smile tugged at her lips at the thought of Gilead. Moriah had never met anyone like him before. He was smart and charismatic and . . . a gift from God.

Not just to her. To everyone. To the world.

The world just didn't realize it yet.

He was the reason Moriah had turned her life around, though. She owed him everything. And, one day, she would give him everything.

Her sandals hit the rocky sand beneath her as she walked toward the water. Though the ocean pounded the other side of the island, Gilead's Cove was located on the shore of the Pamlico Sound. The waters were much more peaceful here, but she'd heard the bugs and snakes could be bad. She'd find out about that when the weather got warmer.

"The Council is waiting," Ruth reminded her, motioning that Moriah should hurry her steps.

She wasn't sure why Ruth had been assigned as her roommate. The woman, tolerable at first, had quickly become overbearing. Moriah couldn't wait until they no longer had to live together.

Love your neighbors because love changes the world.

She remembered the verse from Makir—a book of the Bible Gilead had discovered himself.

It was so hard to put those commands into practice sometimes, though. But she would try, for the sake of the cause. But she felt certain Ruth had been placed in her life as a trial, as a way to cultivate joy in hard times just as the book of James in the Bible talked about.

In the distance, Moriah spotted a fire burning. Six silhouettes stood around it, most likely silent, with their bodies stiff.

The Council.

The sight reminded Moriah of an archaic ritual full of sacred beauty.

"Go, girl," Ruth whispered. "Don't be scared. You'll be fine."

If Moriah would be fine, then why was there a slight quiver to Ruth's voice?

A new fear invaded her.

Just what did this initiation entail?

Moriah sucked in a deep breath of courage and stepped forward. One of the members of the Council—Enoch—reached out his hand for her, and she stepped inside the circle.

This was it. This was when she'd officially become a Makirite.

Her gaze quickly scanned the group of men, and her heart thudded with a new realization. Gilead wasn't here. Moriah had thought he would be, and disappointment bit deep that he was absent.

No, that's okay, Moriah. He trusts his Council to do this, and he doesn't have to be here. It's the sign of a great leader.

Moriah's eyes flickered to another one of the council members. Dietrich. He held something in his hand—it almost looked like a poker.

A poker?

Her heart rate quickened.

What in the world would they use a poker for?

"Thou shall suffer for the cause." Dietrich's voice sounded solemn with ceremony and decorum. "The Dedicated all bear the markings of Makir. In this way, we can be set apart. Do you agree, Moriah? Do you want to be set apart?"

"I do." Her voice trembled at the uncertainties of what she was about to get into, and her eyes didn't leave the glowing, orange metal in Dietrich's hands.

"And do you believe in suffering for the cause?"

"I do." *Consider it pure joy when you face trials of many kinds . . .*

"Then reveal your shoulder," Dietrich said.

Reveal her shoulder? Were they . . . ?

Everyone waited.

Hardly able to breathe, Moriah pulled the tunic down from her left shoulder, exposing her skin to the frigid air.

Dietrich lifted the glowing poker and turned toward her.

"On your knees," he directed.

Her knees? Another tremble rolled through Moriah as all blood left her face.

You can trust these people, Moriah. They're your friends. Your community. Your people.

With one more breath of hesitation, Moriah lowered herself to the ground.

But when she saw the burning hot metal headed toward her, all of her strength and resolve vanished.

What was she doing here? Was this all one big, bad mistake—just like most of the decisions in her life had been?

As the metal hit her skin, a groan emerged from a part of her soul so deep she hadn't even realized it existed. The world around her spun as pain captured her in its entirety and tears spilled down her cheeks.

And, then, as the realization about what was happening reached her brain, she screamed. And screamed. And screamed some more.

ALSO BY CHRISTY BARRITT:

THE LANTERN BEACH MYSTERY SERIES

Hidden Currents

You can take the detective out of the investigation, but you can't take the investigator out of the detective. A notorious gang puts a bounty on Detective Cady Matthews's head after she takes down their leader, leaving her no choice but to hide until she can testify at trial. But her temporary home across the country on a remote North Carolina island isn't as peaceful as she initially thinks. Living under the new identity of Cassidy Livingston, she struggles to keep her investigative skills tucked away, especially after a body washes ashore. When local police bungle the murder investigation, she can't resist stepping in. But Cassidy is supposed to be keeping a low profile. One wrong move could lead to both her discovery and her demise. Can she bring justice to the island . . . or will the hidden currents surrounding her pull her under for good?

Flood Watch

The tide is high, and so is the danger on Lantern Beach. Still in hiding after infiltrating a dangerous gang, Cassidy Livingston just has to make it a few more months before she can testify at trial and resume her old life. But trouble keeps finding her, and Cassidy is pulled into a local investigation after a man mysteriously disappears from the island she now calls home. A recurring nightmare from her time undercover only muddies things, as does a visit from the parents of her handsome ex-Navy SEAL neighbor. When a friend's life is threatened, Cassidy must make choices that put her on the verge of blowing her cover. With a flood watch on her emotions and her life in a tangle, will Cassidy find the truth? Or will her past finally drown her?

Storm Surge

A storm is brewing hundreds of miles away, but its effects are devastating even from afar. Laid-back, loose, and light: that's Cassidy Livingston's new motto. But when a makeshift boat with a bloody cloth inside washes ashore near her oceanfront home, her detective instincts shift into gear . . . again. Seeking clues isn't the only thing on her mind—romance is heating up with next-door neighbor and former Navy SEAL Ty Chambers as well. Her heart wants the love and stability she's longed for her entire life. But her hidden identity only leads to a tidal wave of turbulence. As more answers emerge about the boat, the danger around her rises, creating a treacherous swell that threatens to reveal her past. Can

Cassidy mind her own business, or will the storm surge of violence and corruption that has washed ashore on Lantern Beach leave her life in wreckage?

Dangerous Waters

Danger lurks on the horizon, leaving only two choices: find shelter or flee. Cassidy Livingston's new identity has begun to feel as comfortable as her favorite sweater. She's been tucked away on Lantern Beach for weeks, waiting to testify against a deadly gang, and is settling in to a new life she wants to last forever. When she thinks she spots someone malevolent from her past, panic swells inside her. If an enemy has found her, Cassidy won't be the only one who's a target. Everyone she's come to love will also be at risk. Dangerous waters threaten to pull her into an overpowering chasm she may never escape. Can Cassidy survive what lies ahead? Or has the tide fatally turned against her?

Perilous Riptide

Just when the current seems safer, an unseen danger emerges and threatens to destroy everything. When Cassidy Livingston finds a journal hidden deep in the recesses of her ice cream truck, her curiosity kicks into high gear. Islanders suspect that Elsa, the journal's owner, didn't die accidentally. Her final entry indicates their suspicions might be correct and that what Elsa observed on her final night may have led to her demise. Against the advice of Ty Chambers, her former Navy SEAL boyfriend, Cassidy taps into her detective skills and hunts for answers. But her search only leads to a skeletal body and trouble for both of them. As helplessness threatens to drown her, Cassidy is desperate to turn back time. Can Cassidy find what she needs to navigate the perilous situation? Or will the riptide surrounding her threaten everyone and everything Cassidy loves?

Deadly Undertow

The current's fatal pull is powerful, but so is one detective's will to live. When someone from Cassidy Livingston's past shows up on Lantern Beach and warns her of impending peril, opposing currents collide, threatening to drag her under. Running would be easy. But leaving would break her heart. Cassidy must decipher between the truth and lies, between reality and deception. Even more importantly, she must decide whom to trust and whom to fear. Her life depends on it. As danger rises and answers surface, everything Cassidy thought she knew is tested. In order to survive, Cassidy must take drastic measures and end the battle against the ruthless gang DH-7 once and for all. But if her final mission fails, the consequences will be as deadly as the raging undertow.

Tides of Deception

Change has come to Lantern Beach: a new police chief, a new season, and . . . a new romance? Austin Brooks has loved Skye Lavinia from the moment they met, but the walls she keeps around her seem impenetrable. Skye knows Austin is the best thing to ever happen to her. Yet she also knows that if he learns the truth about her past, he'd be a fool not to run. A chance encounter brings secrets bubbling to the surface, and danger soon follows. Are the life-threatening events plaguing them really accidents . . . or is someone trying to send a deadly message? With the tides on Lantern Beach come deception and lies. One question remains— who will be swept away as the water shifts? And will it bring the end for Austin and Skye, or merely the beginning?

Shadow of Intrigue

For her entire life, Lisa Garth has felt like a supporting character in the drama of life. The designation never bothered her—until now. Lantern Beach, where she's settled and runs a popular restaurant, has boarded up for the season. The slower pace leaves her with too much time alone. Braden Dillinger came to Lantern Beach to try to heal. The former Special Forces officer returned from battle with invisible scars and diminished hope. But his recovery is hampered by the fact that an unknown enemy is trying to kill him. From the moment Lisa and Braden meet, danger ignites around them, and both are drawn into a web of intrigue that turns their lives upside down. As shadows creep in, will Lisa and Braden be able to shine a light on the peril around them? Or will the encroaching darkness turn their worst nightmares into reality?

Storm of Doubt

A pastor who's lost faith in God. A romance writer who's lost faith in love. A faceless man with a deadly obsession. Nothing has felt right in Pastor Jack Wilson's world since his wife died two years ago. He hoped coming to Lantern Beach might help soothe the ragged edges of his soul. Instead, he feels more alone than ever. Novelist Juliette Grace came to the island to hide away. Though her professional life has never been better, her personal life has imploded. Her husband left her and a stalker's threats have grown more and more dangerous. When Jack saves Juliette from an attack, he sees the terror in her gaze and knows he must protect her. But when danger strikes again, will Jack be able to keep her safe? Or will the approaching storm prove too strong to withstand?

YOU MIGHT ALSO ENJOY ...

THE SQUEAKY CLEAN MYSTERY SERIES

On her way to completing a degree in forensic science, Gabby St. Claire drops out of school and starts her own crime-scene cleaning business. When a routine cleaning job uncovers a murder weapon the police overlooked, she realizes that the wrong person is in jail. She also realizes that crime scene cleaning might be the perfect career for utilizing her investigative skills.

#1 Hazardous Duty
#2 Suspicious Minds
#2.5 It Came Upon a Midnight Crime (novella)
#3 Organized Grime
#4 Dirty Deeds
#5 The Scum of All Fears
#6 To Love, Honor and Perish
#7 Mucky Streak
#8 Foul Play
#9 Broom & Gloom

HOLLY ANNA PALADIN MYSTERIES:

When Holly Anna Paladin is given a year to live, she embraces her final days doing what she loves most—random acts of kindness. But when one of her extreme good deeds goes horribly wrong, implicating Holly in a string of murders, Holly is suddenly in a different kind of fight for her life. She knows one thing for sure: she only has a short amount of time to make a difference. And if helping the people she cares about puts her in danger, it's a risk worth taking.

THE WORST DETECTIVE EVER:

I'm not really a private detective. I just play one on TV.

Joey Darling, better known to the world as Raven Remington, detective extraordinaire, is trying to separate herself from her invincible alter ego. She played the spunky character for five years on the hit TV show *Relentless*, which catapulted her to fame and into the role of Hollywood's sweetheart. When her marriage falls apart, her finances dwindle to nothing, and her father disappears, Joey finds herself on the Outer Banks of North Carolina, trying to piece together her life away from the limelight. But as people continually mistake her for the character she played on TV, she's tasked with solving real life crimes . . . even though she's terrible at it.

ABOUT THE AUTHOR

USA Today has called Christy Barritt's books "scary, funny, passionate, and quirky."

Christy writes both mystery and romantic suspense novels that are clean with underlying messages of faith. Her books have won the Daphne du Maurier Award for Excellence in Suspense and Mystery, have been twice nominated for the Romantic Times Reviewers' Choice Award, and have finaled for both a Carol Award and Foreword Magazine's Book of the Year.

She is married to her Prince Charming, a man who thinks she's hilarious—but only when she's not trying to be. Christy is a self-proclaimed klutz, an avid music lover who's known for spontaneously bursting into song, and a road trip aficionado.

When she's not working or spending time with her family, she enjoys singing, playing the guitar, and exploring small, unsuspecting towns where people have no idea how accident-prone she is.

Find Christy online at:

www.christybarritt.com
www.facebook.com/christybarritt
www.twitter.com/cbarritt

Sign up for Christy's newsletter to get information on all of her latest releases here: **www.christybarritt.com/newsletter-sign-up/**

If you enjoyed this book, please consider leaving a review.

50187191R00179

Made in the USA
Middletown, DE
23 June 2019